THE GHOST
IN THE WOOD

Also by Marianne Mitchell

Finding Zola

Firebug

Windows of Gold

A Promise Made

A ghost tale for you, Emma

THE GHOST
IN THE WOOD

MARIANNE MITCHELL

Marianne Mitchell

RAFTER FIVE PRESS

Cover illustration by Christopher Elwell, Dreamstime
Cover Design by Sinonda Enterprises

Published by Rafter Five Press
Tucson, Arizona

ISBN: 978-0-9673497-5-6

To my brother, Stan Olson...

...who gave me the load
of lightning-struck wood
that inspired this story

THEN.....

The wind roared up the canyon that afternoon, whipping dry cottonwood leaves into dancing whirls of yellow. Dark clouds rolled in soon after, tumbling over the mountains and bringing deeper and deeper rumbles of thunder.

In a small cabin near the Rustic River, a young boy and his father leaned over a checkerboard, studying their next moves by the yellow glow of a kerosene lamp. The boy's hand hovered in circles over the board, undecided, until an explosion of light and sound split the air. He leaped up, dumping the checkerboard and scattering the red and black discs across the floor.

His face paled, remembering the fight he'd had that afternoon with Joey, his best friend. It was some stupid argument about sharing comic books. When Joey refused to lend him his newest Superman issue, he'd climbed down from the tree fort in a huff and left. He'd meant to come back. Really he had.

"Cripes!" he whispered, heading for the door. "I forgot about him."

"Where do ya think you're goin'?" yelled his father.

"Joey's still out there. I gotta go."

Heart pounding, he darted outside. Rain poured off the tin roof, soaking him instantly. Splashing through puddles, he ran down the path toward the river. The rain quickly turned to hail, pelting him with stinging beads of ice. As more lightning flashed, he scanned the tree line for one special tree. It should have been easy to spot because it was shaped like the letter Y, as if it had decided to be two trees instead of one after it grew from the earth. The boys had hauled old wooden planks from the garage all the way down to the river to build their special hideout. High enough in the branches for a good view, but easy enough to reach with a ladder.

Now, everything around him was outlined in electric blue with an intense smoky odor in the mist. But it wasn't the comforting pine smoke from the cabin's stovepipe. This was acrid, burnt, with a tinge of sulfur. The putrid smell grew as he neared the tree which no longer looked like the letter Y. Instead, a blackened gash had split the trunk and its once sturdy branches now lay in sizzling chunks across the ground along with charred planks from the tree house. The grass steamed in a wide circle around the stump of the tree, tracing the pattern of the roots underground. And amid the shattered ruins, pages from comic books drooped on the wet grass, their curled edges singed. The ladder was the only thing spared. It lay off in the bushes where he had dragged it after the fight. Far enough away so Joey'd be stuck up there.

Stuck with no way to get down.

.....fifty years later

CHAPTER 1

"Are we there yet?"

My sister Robbyn had asked this about a bazillion times.

"Soon, Toots," Dad replied.

She sat back and tugged on her two ponytails, her mouth pulled down in a pout.

I craned my neck, looking up the highway for the turn-off marking the driveway to Almosta Ranch. Great Aunt Sara had explained that it wasn't really a ranch, just *almost a ranch*, har-har. It was a log cabin on the Rustic River with a few acres rented out for horses. Her family sometimes used the place as a vacation spot for a few weeks in the summer.

We were heading there because Dad lost his job six months ago and he'd run out of savings to keep paying rent on our condo in Phoenix. He'd even spent all the money from insurance after Mom had died. At first, Dad turned down Aunt Sara's offer of the cabin in Colorado. He kept telling her things would get better. But somehow she convinced him he'd be doing her a favor by staying there. Having someone around would keep curious hikers away and give it a real lived-in look, she'd said. Dad finally agreed on the condition that she let him fix up the place, get it winterized so the family could use it all year.

"It'll be an adventure!" Dad had explained when he told me and Robbyn about the plan. "Better than camping because we'll have a real house. Work in exchange for rent. Whaddya say?"

"Are we moving all our stuff?" I asked.

"Most of our things will go into storage for a while, Zeke. But no need to worry. The cabin is furnished; pots, pans, linens and all. We just bring our clothes. You and Robbyn can take one box each of toys and books."

Robbyn hugged her teddy bear. "Can Bear go?"

"He sure can, Toots. He'll love the forest."

With that, she ran off, looking for other toys to take along.

"What about the TV?" I asked. "Can I take my computer?"

"Nope. And nope. I'm taking my laptop but only for writing."

I groaned. "How far out in the woods is this place? Does it even have electricity?"

"It does. But we'll be in a canyon and Aunt Sara said there's no TV or cell phone reception there. The cabin has a land line and the radio works—sometimes. Internet connection is only dial-up and even that's spotty."

A stay in prison sounded like more fun. I'd be out in the sticks with none of my friends or comforts of life. While Dad packed up what we could take and arranged to put the rest in storage, I played catch against the side of the house. With every *thwack!* I thought about how moving meant I'd miss the rest of the baseball season with the Gila Monsters. Not that I'd get much play since I'd been suspended for five games over a fight with my ex-friend Taylor. He'd been suspended, too, and blamed me for the whole mess—a dumb argument about a bad call at the plate. And it got worse. Come fall I'd be starting seventh grade in a new school. Robbyn and I would have an hour bus ride down the canyon to get there. That should be loads of fun when it's winter with ice and snow.

We had stopped for groceries in town before heading up the canyon. Aunt Sara had warned us to stock up because the little store at Rustic only carried a few basics. The road was scenic but twisty, following a river that tumbled and churned over rocks and around sharp bends. At times the river looked more like dark root beer than plain mountain water.

For miles the hillsides along the canyon were bare and black. Burned trees reached to the sky like scrawny fingers.

"What happened?" asked Robbyn.

"Forest fire," said Dad. "Last summer over fifty thousand acres burned. Aunt Sara said it was caused by a campfire. The firefighters stopped it long before it got to the cabin." He pointed to the river water. "See how black it runs? That's from all the ash."

Farther on, the hills were green again and the water ran clear. We slowed down as we passed old school busses unloading people in wet suits eager to ride the rapids while their guides toted bright yellow rafts down to the river's edge. I wanted to jump out of the van and climb into one of those rafts and go back home. Except we didn't have a home anymore. Just some crummy cabin in the wilderness.

"Nearly there," Dad said. He flashed me a grin which was supposed to make me feel better. It didn't. "We just passed mile marker ninety-one. Look for ninety-three. The driveway should be soon after on the left with a sign for Almosta Ranch"

"I have to go potty," whined Robbyn.

"You just went ten minutes ago," I reminded her. "Jeez, you're almost six years old. Hold on a little longer. I'm sure the cabin has a clean potty, not like that smelly old one back at the rest stop."

Robbyn pinched her nose. "I didn't use it. It was icky."

A couple of miles later, Dad pointed to a sign. "There it is—Almosta Ranch."

He slowed and turned off onto a dirt drive blocked by a wide metal gate. A weathered wood sign dangled from a strand of barbed wire. Long ago the paint had worn off in places so now the sign simply read:

ALMOST RAN

Not a good omen.

I hopped out and swung the gate wide so Dad could pass on through. As I hooked the gate closed again, I gazed down the drive. Weeds and overgrown grass nearly covered the faint track heading toward the river. A half-dozen horses stopped their grazing in the field to stare at us newcomers. I climbed back in the van and Dad eased ahead slowly, steering around ruts when he saw them in time, bouncing into them when he didn't. At the end of the drive, a cluster of tall cottonwoods surrounded an old brown cabin and several small outbuildings.

"Are you sure this is the place Aunt Sara meant?" I asked.

Dad nodded. "Yup. It'll look fine once we get out the weed whacker and get it cleaned up. It's been vacant all winter."

It looked like it had been vacant a lot longer than that.

When Dad pulled up in front of the cabin, I wasn't in any hurry to get out. Up close it looked even worse than from the gate. Dry leaves had piled in heaps by the door and worn steps led up to a sagging front porch. The screen door hung limply from a broken frame that was marked with long scratches, as if some wild animal had tried to get inside. The log siding, which hinted that it was once painted dark brown, was now faded and peeling. Yellowed window shades blocked any views inside.

"I have to pee," wailed Robbyn. She jumped out of the van and ran up the steps to the door. "Open it, Daddy!"

Dad laughed. "This way, my dear."

He gestured toward a tiny log hut about fifty feet from the cabin. "Aunt Sara says it's the prettiest outhouse on the river."

I sighed. An outhouse. Great. No TV. No indoor plumbing.

Robbyn scampered over and peered inside. "Eeeew!" But she went in anyway. She must have really had to go.

CHAPTER 2

Inside, the cabin wasn't too awful. It didn't smell bad and looked more or less clean. Half the cabin was one long room with a kitchen at one end and a table and chairs at the other. An old cast-iron potbellied stove hugged the wall in the middle. Faded linoleum decorated in a funky block pattern covered the floor. The rest of the floors were bare wood. At least the kitchen had a working electric stove and a refrigerator. The other half off the main room had two bedrooms, one for Dad and one with bunk beds for Robbyn and me.

Robbyn hopped on the bottom bunk. "Mine!" she cried.

"No problem. I wanted the top anyway," I said. I tossed my backpack on the upper bunk sending puffs of dust everywhere.

While Robbyn pulled clothes and her teddy bear out of her suitcase, I helped Dad bring in the bags of groceries we'd bought. Aunt Sara had arranged for a handyman to get the electricity turned on and the pump started. A pipe from the pump house brought the only running water to a spigot out on the porch.

"See?" Dad said, turning it on and letting water gush into a kettle. "Much better than carrying water up from the river. We'll keep this kettle filled and on the stove for hot water."

"What about showers?" I asked.

Dad shook his head. "Not here. There are showers and laundry facilities up at the campground we can use."

"How can you be so upbeat?" I asked, spreading out my arms. "This is like going back in time, back before civilization."

"It's not quite that bad," said Dad. "And I really need your support in this move, Zeke. It won't be forever, I promise."

Robbyn came out to the porch hugging her teddy bear. "Bear wants to go outside," she announced. "He wants to find other bears."

I glanced out to the trees surrounding the cabin. "Are there bears around here?"

Dad pointed to the long scratches on the door. "Who do you think made those?"

"Great," I moaned. "Bears breaking in to eat us."

Robbyn's eyes widened as she peered out from her bangs. "N-not eat us!"

Dad gave her a hug. "He's just teasing, aren't you Zeke? The bears are way up in the mountains munching on berries now. Those scratches were probably made in the spring when they woke up hungry."

Robbyn didn't look convinced. The screen door not only had long scratches, but the frame was badly bent. I could picture a huge bear swatting the door with his paw, trying to get inside.

Dad studied the wooden frame. "This can be fixed once I get it off. A few nails, a little wood glue and it will be good as new. While I work on this, how about you show Robbyn that swing I saw down by the river."

That brought a smile to her freckled face.

I shrugged out a sigh and led her to a tall cottonwood tree that stood halfway between the cabin and the river. Sure enough, a rope swing with a smooth wooden seat hung from a long branch. I tested the strength of the ropes, hoping they hadn't rotted out. Then I hoisted Robbyn onto the seat and gave her a push.

"Higher!" she cried.

After a few good pushes, she was pumping on her own, her ponytails blowing back in the breeze.

Soft burbles from the river drew me down to the rocky bank. The fishy-smelling water was running low now, but it must have been lots higher in the spring. Out in the center of the stream, small branches and other debris had caught in the rocks of a low island. I thought it would be easy to wade across until I swished my hand in the water. Yikes it was cold! Maybe not.

Robbyn was still swinging, slower now, but she looked happy enough. I wandered across the grassy yard, stopping to swipe dead leaves off a weathered old picnic table. Under the boughs of the cottonwoods grew a dozen blue spruce pines. When the wind blew, it smelled a little like Christmas.

Besides the outhouse and pump house, the only other building was a detached garage. It looked like it had once been a cabin, too, but now one end held two enormous doors closed with a rusty padlock.

Disappointed, I gave the lock a tug. Something gave a bit. I tugged harder. The wood was so rotten it crumbled and the lock came off in my hand, still firmly closed.

"Sweet!"

The door creaked open revealing a long interior. I eased inside, letting my eyes adjust to the darkness. My brain tried to puzzle out what the strange shapes lurking in the corners were. Dust and mold tickled my nose, making me sneeze. Something scuttled under papers stacked on the floor, startling me. *Relax, dummy!* It was probably just a mouse. I rubbed my arms against the cold, heavy air in the garage. It was like stepping into a walk-in freezer.

By now I could make out some glass canning jars on the shelves, fishing rods and rakes up in the rafters, a bunch of tools on a wooden work bench, boxes of old National Geographic magazines and a stack of car tires in the back. Best of all, a rust-speckled bicycle leaned against a pile of wood, half hidden under a plastic tarp. I pulled back the tarp, knocking a couple of logs off the woodpile as I did. A whisper of cold air brushed my legs, making me shiver even more as I inspected the bike.

Both tires were flat, of course. I glanced back at the workbench. Yes! One of the tools was a tire pump. After filling the old tires with what I hoped was enough air, I was about to wheel the bike outside when a high-pitched scream cut through the air.

CHAPTER 3

"Why did you push me off?" Robbyn cried. She sat like a lump on the ground, the swing dancing wildly around her.

"I didn't touch you. I was in the garage, way over there."

She stuck out her lip. "Somebody pushed me."

"You just slipped off the seat, that's all."

"No I didn't." She got up and brushed the dirt and grass from her arms and legs. "I'm telling Daddy."

"Fine. Be a baby."

"I'm not a baby!"

Dad strode down the steps frowning. "What's the ruckus out here?"

"Zeke pushed me off the swing."

"I did not. I wasn't anywhere near her."

Dad gave Robbyn a hug. "Are you hurt?"

"No," she blubbered.

"Keep an eye on her, Zeke. We're a long ways from a doctor here if one of us gets hurt." He ruffled Robbyn's hair. "And you be careful on that swing, OK?"

I groaned. Instead of taking my newfound bike for a spin, I was saddled with watching over my kid sister. Again. The trouble with having a sibling six years younger is that you almost never like doing the same things. Plus, she was a girl. When Mom brought her home from the hospital it was a real let down. I'd hoped for a brother, someone already old enough to play with me. The fact that babies arrived so small ruined all my plans.

I propped the bike against the garage with a sigh. It was only our first day. There'd be other days I could go for a ride and Robbyn needed cheering up.

"Let's go down to the river. We can throw sticks in the water and see how far they float."

A grin replaced her pout. There was hope for this kid.

We followed a footpath that cut through some weeds and scrub brush until we came to a small sandy beach where the river widened and ran much calmer. The way the sun sparkled off the water made me wish we'd put on sunscreen before starting out. Robbyn started picking up small sticks and rocks to throw in the water while I wandered a few yards upstream to a wooded area looking for some stubby pieces of wood. We could toss them into the river and pretend they were battleships to sink.

But as I headed back to the beach with my arms full, the shadows from the trees seemed to follow me, their long, dark arms reaching out closer and closer to me. Stepping back onto the sunny beach, I shook off the idea of shadows chasing me and got our 'battleships' launched into the river.

The 'battle' ended when Robbyn saw a pretty rock in the water and waded out to get it. She slipped, of course, and got soaked. I whipped off my T-shirt and tried to dry her but still she shivered.

"We better get back," I told her.

Dad didn't scold but I could tell from the scowl on his face he was not happy with me. Robbyn was not only wet, but her fair skin was pink from sunburn. Mine not so bad.

"The sun is stronger up here," he explained. "You've got to take it easy." He smeared aloe cream on us to ease the sting, just like Mom used to do when I got a scrape.

Mom died a couple of years after Robbyn was born so Dad had been both parents to us. He did OK but I helped with cleaning, doing laundry and watching my sister. At first, Dad didn't know anything about cooking so we ate out or had take-out pizza at home. But that got expensive. Then Dad got into studying recipes on the Internet and using us as guinea pigs. He had a science background so to him all recipes were 'formulas.' There were some flops, but in the end he turned out to be a pretty good cook and he never blew up the kitchen. Something smelled delicious tonight.

"Tuna hot dish in twenty minutes," Dad announced when he finished with our first-aid.

"Yay! My favorite!" said Robbyn. She got napkins and salt and pepper shakers from the cabinet.

"Help her set the table, Zeke."

"I saw some fishing poles in the garage today," I said, grabbing some silverware from a drawer. "Maybe we can catch some trout."

"You're on. But first I need to take stock of what needs to be done with this place. I promised Aunt Sara I'd fix it up. You can help, too. The sooner we get the cabin in tip top shape, the sooner I can get back to my book."

Dad had been working on his book for ages, something about microbes locked in the meteors that hit the earth. He hoped that getting it published would also help him land another teaching job at a university. I thought getting a job should come first, but I tried to stay positive for his sake.

While Dad checked on the casserole, I fiddled with the radio on the kitchen table. Reception was lousy. Cowboy music, farm reports, some guy ranting about politics, and lots of static. I missed TV. I missed my computer. I missed texting my friends. We'd probably never find out if giant transformers from the planet Xeron invaded America while we were stuck here. Rats.

CHAPTER 4

As soon as the sun set, the temperature dropped like a skydiver. Dad reminded us we were at an elevation of over 7,000 feet. He gave the old potbellied stove a pat.

"I bet this baby warms the place up in no time." He checked the wood box beside the stove. "Hm. Empty. See if you can hustle up some kindling outside, Zeke. Take the flashlight."

I knew right where to look for firewood. I'd seen a pile of it in the garage under the tarp. The garage door creaked again as I opened but this time I was prepared for it. And for the scurry of little mice feet. The flashlight beam bounced around the frigid interior until I located the old woodpile. I dumped some magazines out of a cardboard box and started filing it with chunks of wood. They looked charred and smelled musty. As I lugged the box into the cabin, I hoped they'd still burn.

20

"Great. You found some! The flue is open and the insides look clean." Dad sat cross-legged on the floor scrunching up wads of newspaper into the stove.

I dumped my load into the wood box. "I don't know, Dad. This wood looks awfully old. Who knows how long it's been out in that garage. Some pieces look like they'd already been in a fire."

"Dry wood should burn fine." He used a small hatchet to chop up pieces of kindling. Those he stacked around the newspaper wads inside the stove. "We'll soon find out." He struck a match and lit the papers.

Flames licked up the sides of the kindling sending snapping sparks up the stovepipe. Once the kindling was really burning, Dad added two bigger pieces of wood. But as they caught fire, a dark, acrid smoke began to billow out into the room.

"Are you sure the flue was open?" I asked, coughing and waving my hands in the air. Smoke stung my eyes as it rolled across the room like a dark cloud.

"Positive." Dad tapped the tall stovepipe again. "It's not drawing right," he said. "Robbyn, open the door for some fresh air."

She ran to open the door as I stumbled through the haze to get a window open. Pots and pans tumbled off the worktable. I didn't think I'd bumped it, but it was hard to tell where furniture was in all the smoke. Then Robbyn cried out.

"Look, Daddy! A smoke person!"

Gray swirls of smoke now floated from the potbellied stove, not diffused like normal smoke anymore, but shaped like a human form as if the air currents were sculpting it. Then, pulsing as if it were alive, the smoke slipped out the screen door and the fire in the stove sputtered out.

"Bye-bye smoke," said Robbyn with a wave.

Weird. But at least the air was clear again. And freezing cold. I shut the window fast before we lost all the heat in the room. As Robbyn shoved the door closed, I stared back at Dad.

He acted as if he hadn't seen anything odd except a lot of smoke. He tapped the stovepipe with his knuckles. "Maybe there's a bird's nest up top. I'll climb on the roof tomorrow and check it out. We have to do without heat tonight."

Normal. How could he be so normal? Didn't Robbyn and I see something that was definitely not normal? Was the altitude playing tricks on our eyes? I shook my head. It must have been the wind that swirled up the smoke. Nothing else made sense.

Getting ready for bed at the cabin was more of a chore than it had been at home. Dishes were done by hand with hot water poured from the kettle on the electric stove. All traces of food had to be thrown away or stowed in the big white cabinet. Aunt Sara had warned us that mice were a problem in the cabin so Dad set the mousetraps in case we had any little visitors. We washed up and brushed our teeth out on the porch where the water spigot was. I had to escort Robbyn to the outhouse because she was too chicken to go alone down the dark path.

And of course she wanted a story before going to sleep. Dad was working on his book so the job fell to me. I got her into her bunk then climbed up on my own.

"There once was a princess named..."

"Robbyn!"

"...named Robbyn. But her real name was Serena Sleepyhead. A wicked witch had cast a spell on her that made her fall asleep every time she heard the word 'apple.' Since her father owned an apple orchard, he was always talking about the apple crop and Serena was always falling asleep.

'We have to do something!' said the king. So he sent for his brave knight, Sir Arfer, who was really a dog. 'Fetch me the wicked witch so she can undo her spell,' commanded the king. So the dog ran off and found the witch. But while he was dragging her back to the palace, she vanished in a puff of smoke."

"Maybe she's the smoke person now," said Robbyn.

"Right. And because she was no longer a witch, the evil spell was broken and the princess lived apple-ly ever after."

"That's silly," she said with a wide yawn.

"G'night Robbie."

"Nite-nite."

Snug in our bunk beds, I listened as Robbyn's breathing turned to a gentle snore. We were all tired from the move up here and the change in altitude. But for me it was too quiet. I missed the hum of traffic from our old neighborhood, the barking of our neighbor's dog, and the glow from the street lamp outside my window. Here, I only heard the soft shush of the pine trees. My eyelids grew heavy and I finally sank into sleep.

When I woke, hours later, it was still dark and eerily quiet. No sound had pulled me out of sleep. Instead, it was a strong odor, like rotten eggs. I propped myself up on my elbows and sniffed. Gas companies put a sulfur smell in the gas lines so if there's a leak, you'll notice it. But nothing in the cabin needed gas, so it couldn't have been a gas leak. Something shadowy outside moved by the window. I pulled back the thin curtain and caught my breath.

Blue gray smoke swirled and twisted just out in the yard, turning its wispy trails into the shape of arms and legs, then a misshapen head. Ghostly hands reached out to me as if beckoning me to come join him. Thin wisps of smoke brushed the windowpanes and seeped under the sash bringing in the rotten egg smell.

"Ahhh!" I jerked myself back, coughing on the smoke. How could the smoke still be hanging around? Had the fire restarted in the potbellied stove? Panicked, I darted out into the main room to check. All was dark and calm. The refrigerator

24

hummed softly. A yellow recharge light glowed from Dad's laptop. The side of the potbellied stove was cool to my touch. With no fire, how could there be smoke? I went to the door and peeked through its small window but saw nothing on the pitch-black porch or in the yard. Feeling silly that I must have let a dream about smoky ghosts trick me, I stumbled back to my bunk and fell into a deep sleep.

CHAPTER 5

When the phone rang the next morning, Dad was up on the roof so I answered. It was Aunt Sara.

"How are you doing?" she asked. "Getting all settled?"

"Yeah. It takes some getting used to, you know, with no indoor plumbing. And no Internet. At least there's electricity so Dad can use his laptop for writing."

"You'll find other things to do. There are books and games on the bookshelf and a box of craft stuff in the closet. Also, the gal who boards the horses will be stopping by. Maybe she can take you and Robbyn on a trail ride. How's Matt coming with his book?"

"Um, he's up on the roof right now checking the stovepipe. We tried to have a fire in the

26

potbellied stove last night and the room filled with smoke. He thought there might be a bird's nest blocking the flue."

"I don't think so. I had my handyman check all that before you got there. It was working fine."

"Then maybe it was the wood we used. I found it in the garage."

Aunt Sara didn't respond right away. "Hmm. In the garage? Oh, I know the wood you mean. It's been there for ages. Years ago my father cut up an old lightning-struck tree and we piled the wood in the garage. I don't think we ever used any of it, though. Pine logs burned so much better."

"That wood's no good anyway." I paused. Her answer explained part of our problem, but there must be more to the story. "Was the tree near the cabin when it was hit?"

"No, it was down by the river. There's a sad story about that tree. A young boy was up in it when it was hit."

"Was he hurt?"

"He was killed instantly."

The back of my neck prickled. Visions of a kid up a tree in a lightning storm flashed in my mind. What an awful way to die! "Do you think there's anything left of that tree?"

"Maybe. It's been a long time, Zeke. Follow the footpath to a wooded area near a little beach. The tree was near there, I think."

"Thanks. I know where that is. I'll let you know what I find."

Just then, Dad tromped into the cabin. "No nest. The pipe's all clear."

I held the phone out to him. "It's Aunt Sara."

He plunked himself down at the table to chat.

Out on the porch Robbyn sat gluing sticks and moss on rocks. "I'm making a rock family," she said as I skipped down the steps.

"Neat. They look like forest trolls."

"Uh-huh. Where are you going?"

"Not far. You can show me the whole family when I get back."

I was glad she didn't want to come along. Finding that stump was something I had to do alone. The footpath was easy to follow since yesterday Robbyn and I had tromped down the weeds. But today I went farther along, following a barbed wire fence that ran along the field where the horses were kept. When I neared the woods, I ducked under the barbed wire and threaded my way through an aspen grove. Taller trees loomed ahead.

I turned around, scanning the area for anything that looked like an old tree stump. The beavers had been busy leaving their gnaw marks on small aspen and downing a bunch more. In between the rocks, tall grass and snaky vines covered old logs so well I thought the only way I'd find the stump was to trip over it. I picked up a river-washed stick and poked through the vegetation. Nothing.

Why would a kid be up in a tree? Did he have a fort? I lifted my eyes to a row of tall cottonwoods bordering the aspen grove. They had strong, spreading branches, perfect for building a tree fort. If I were going to build a tree fort, it would be in one of those, with a great view of the river.

A chill wind came up as I neared the cotton-woods, making me rub the goose bumps that rose on my arms. Something rustled in the bushes behind me and I turned to see what it was. Nothing. Was I being followed? Dad had talked about bears coming from the mountains. Were bears tromping around in the woods now?

Another sound came, a deep rumbly noise. My pulse quickened and my steps hurried through the brush. Long shadows surrounded me as sharp branches caught on my jeans and twigs snapped. Then suddenly, there it was. The stump. It sat like a jagged throne, its seat a rotted core filled with leaves. What was left of the outer wood was charred black, like the wood in the garage. No grass or weeds grew near it, as if the ground itself was poisoned.

A boy died there. I stared upward, trying again to imagine being up in the tall tree in a thunder-storm, getting zapped by lightning. Getting blown to bits. I hoped he didn't feel anything.

Another stick snapped in the grass, inter-rupting my thoughts. I froze. Suddenly, I was all too aware that someone or something was right behind me. I could feel its hot breath on my neck.

Was it the boy's ghost? Was it a bear? My stomach clenched. My mouth went dry. I wanted to run but my legs had turned to jelly. Then something pushed me from behind, making me stagger forward and fall face first into the dead leaves of the rotten old stump. Twisting around to see who had bumped me, I stared into the dark eyes of a huge animal.

THE GHOST IN THE WOOD

CHAPTER 6

A jet black horse whickered at me like he was asking what the heck I was doing sprawled in the leaves.

I exhaled in relief and hauled myself up. "You scared me, you dumb old horse!" He blinked his big brown eyes and nudged me again with his nose. "How did you get out of the field? Come on. Let's go back."

The horse turned and led the way back to a place where the fence had been trampled down. Two other horses waited there munching on grass. After getting the black horse back into the field, I pulled up the fence post up so they'd be discouraged from breaking out again. Dad could do a better job later.

With one last glance back where the old tree had been, I hurried across the field to the

31

cabin. Now that I'd seen the stump, I had even more questions than before. Was the boy alone when it happened? How did people know he'd been up in the tree? Where was his family? My brain was locked onto the story like a laser beam. Maybe coming to Colorado wasn't going to be so boring after all.

After lunch, Dad checked the tools in the garage and didn't find the kind of pliers he needed to fix the fence. "Guess it's time to see what the little store up at Rustic has to offer," he said. "Maybe we can get some ice cream for dessert."

That was enough to get Robbyn to leave her rock family and jump into the van.

Rustic Resort was anything but a resort. Maybe it had been once, judging by the huge neon sign of a leaping rainbow trout out by the road. It mainly consisted of a tiny café called Rainbow's End and a general store fronting a half-dozen dowdy cabins along the river.

In the store, Dad studied the shelves filled with hardware and fishing gear. Robbyn went straight for the ice cream freezer in the grocery section.

"I want a double fudge cone," she said, poking through the choices.

"Here's one." I handed her the wrapped cone then grabbed an ice cream sandwich for myself.

"You're the folks renting Sara's cabin, right?" asked the clerk when I paid for the ice creams. She reminded me of my grandma. Same gray hair, same smile lines around her brown eyes. Only Grandma wore silky dresses and this lady was dressed in khaki pants and a flannel shirt.

"Yeah. We are. How did you know?"

"Fred told us. He's the handyman who got the place up and running before you all arrived." She handed me my change. "By the way, I'm Anabelle. Everything OK over there?"

"Well, some fencing in the field is down. A horse got out this afternoon so my dad is looking for the right tools to fix it." I nodded in Dad's direction. An older man dressed in overalls and a plaid shirt was showing him a tool kit.

"Vern, he don't need to buy that," said Anabelle. "Give Fred a call and have him do the job. That's what he's paid for."

Vern gave her a salute. "Okey-dokey." He grinned at my dad. "That's my first wife. She keeps me on my toes and this place running."

"I'm your only wife, ya old coot!" she tossed back at him.

"Nice set-up you've got here," said Dad. "A bit of everything. Groceries, hardware, knick-knacks." He nodded at an oil painting of a fish leaping from the water. "That's very colorful."

Vern chuckled. "That's my hobby. Can't go fishin' no more on account of my bad knees, so I paint 'em instead."

"Where does this fellow Fred live?" asked Dad. "I hope he doesn't have to make a long trip just to fix a fence. I can probably take care of it."

"He lives out back in one of the cabins. I'll give him a call and he can meet you at your place. That is, if he's in a decent mood today."

Anabelle flashed Vern a warning look, like maybe Vern shouldn't have let that snarky comment slip to us newcomers.

Fred showed up about a half hour later, his battered red pickup bouncing along the dirt driveway. He looked about sixty, weathered skin, salt and pepper hair tucked under a frayed cowboy hat. He tugged at the brim as he greeted my dad.

"Vern tells me you got some barbed wire fencing down. Whereabouts?"

Dad jerked his head my way. "Zeke can show you. He's the one that spotted it."

"C'mon then. Let's get to it." He hefted a toolbox from his truck.

We tromped along the footpath and cut across the horse pasture. His strides were long and I had to hurry to keep up with him. He didn't chat with me but I was full of questions.

"Do you know much about this place? I mean, like what it was like in the old days?"

He nodded. "Hung around here as a boy."

"Must have been fun, with the river near and lots of trees to climb."

He kept on walking, his boots crushing the tall grass but stepping around all the horse droppings on the way.

I kept after him, hoping he'd share some stories. "You see, I was down here looking for that tree that got zapped by lightning a long time ago. I found it, too. Do you know anything about it?"

He shrugged. Not much of a talker, this guy.

We found the spot where the fence sagged and he got right to work. I helped steady the post while he tightened the barbed wire. The horses sauntered over to watch us. I gave the black one a pat. "Hello, buddy. You scared the daylights out of me today."

Fred looked up. "What'd he do?"

"I'd fallen into that old tree stump, thinking about the kid who died there. The horse came up behind me and gave me a poke. I thought it was the ghost of the dead kid coming after me."

"Ain't no such thing as ghosts," muttered Fred. "That kid wouldn't hurt nobody. Dead or alive."

"So what happened?"

"Accident, that's all."

"Why was he up in the tree in a storm?"

Fred kept working the post, not answering as he tightened the barbed wire until the fence looked as good as new. Straightening up, he gazed in the direction of the tree stump. A frown deepened the lines in his face and he swiped his hand across his brow, like he was trying to wipe away a bad memory. "It was a long time ago. No point in stirring up the past."

I could take a hint. But I wasn't going to stop asking questions until I figured out what happened.

CHAPTER 7

"Who wants hot dogs for dinner?" Dad dangled a package of buns in one hand and a package of dogs in the other.

"I do!" cried Robbyn, jumping up from the unicorn puzzle spread out on the floor.

"You'll join us, won't you, Didi?" Dad asked.

"Thanks, sounds good." Tall and muscular, with chocolate skin, Didi looked every inch a cowgirl. Dusty jeans, boots, checkered shirt and a bandana around her neck completed the picture. She was a vet student at the university and part-time horse wrangler in the summer. The six horses in the fields were hers and she'd stopped by to unload some hay and check the water in their trough.

"Zeke, put some logs in the fire pit outside. We'll cook dinner there with s'mores for dessert."

"I'll help," said Didi, following me out the door.

A circle of smooth river rocks marked the fire pit just off the front porch. Didi piled a bunch of twigs and dry leaves in the center while I loaded up on the pine branches that Dad had cut into small logs.

"I wanted to thank you for your quick action today about the downed fence. Those horses will take any excuse to go wandering. Fred get it all fixed?"

"Yeah, it only took him a few minutes. Your black horse was the one that got out."

"That's Noche. He's always curious about people." She struck a match to the leaves. The fire snapped and crackled, sending small sparks into the dusky sky.

"I love the spicy smell of pine," Didi said, sitting back on her heels.

I nodded. "Way better than those stinky cottonwood logs in the garage. They came from a tree that was hit by lightning."

"No wonder they didn't burn well."

"I think they're haunted."

She tilted her head and looked at me. "Seriously? Why do you say that?"

"Because years ago a kid was in the tree when it got blasted. Now, when we burn the wood, an eerie smoke comes out."

Her eyebrows went up. "How cool. A real ghost haunting."

"Dad says he didn't see anything weird. But he looks at the world with the eyes of a scientist. 'Science can explain everything,' he always says."

"Maybe not everything."

Conversation stopped when Dad and Robbyn came out bringing buns, hot dogs and mustard. I got up and pulled the garden hose over in case a spark jumped the fire pit.

"Are you planning on staying here through the winter?" Didi asked Dad.

"Yup. At least until I find a job."

"What kind of job?"

"I was a chemistry teacher at a college back home. But funding for our program got cut and so did I."

"You know, my sister teaches at the middle school in town and she says they need a science teacher for the coming school year. It'd be a change from university life, but you might like it. In years past, the sixth graders competed in the Science Olympiad."

Dad poked the fire, spreading out the coals. "Maybe so. I'll think about that."

"Dad invents stuff," I added. "Tell her about the shampoo you made."

He laughed. "Just mixed some Castille soap and coconut oil. It worked fine until I got too creative and added some color."

"I had pink hair," said Robbyn, grinning.

"We'll do purple next time," said Dad.

Now that the fire had died down a bit, we stuck hot dogs on long barbecue forks and watched them sizzle. Everything tasted better over an open flame. Maybe it reminded our taste buds of the good old cave man days of roasting wild beasts.

After a couple of dogs, Didi stood up, brushed off her jeans and shook Dad's hand. "Thanks for supper, Matt. I gotta hit the road."

"No dessert?" he asked.

"Another time." She chucked me on the arm and winked. "Let me know if anything goes bump in the night."

I watched her drive off feeling grateful she hadn't said anything to Dad about our ghost talk. His logical scientific mind would never buy into the idea of haunted wood. At least Didi didn't think I was a nut case.

We finished supper with s'mores like Dad had promised. As I munched on gooey toasted marshmallows and chocolate, all smooshed between graham crackers, my thoughts drifted back to the pile of charred wood in the garage. The last time we used it, the cabin filled with smoke. Robbyn had said the smoke looked like a person. And the smoke outside my window that night had looked kinda human, too. Unless that was all just a dream.

Maybe it was time to try my own experiment. A study in 'cause and effect.' Would we have the same weird smoke if I put one of those logs on our campfire? Would it prove the wood was haunted?

We were outside now, so there was no danger of smoking up the cabin.

When Dad took the rest of our food back into the cabin, I ducked into the garage and grabbed one of the old charred pieces of wood. Robbyn had moved over to the cabin steps to play with her teddy bear and rock family so the coast was clear. The coals in the fire pit were gray and ashy, but still hot enough to burn. I tossed the wood onto the coals and sat down to see what happened. At once the log began to hiss and sputter, shooting sparks out onto the dry grass. Dry wood shouldn't spark like that but in seconds a small fire was spreading across the grass.

"Geez!" I ran to the spigot on the porch and turned on the hose.

"Daddy! Zeke is playing with fire," yelled Robbyn.

Dad came out as I was spraying water on the fast spreading flames. And yes, there was smoke. Tons of it, like a dense fog swallowing up everything. I couldn't see the hose in my hand, let alone anything else. When the fire was out, it had left a blackened patch about ten feet long and three feet wide.

"That was close," sighed Dad, stomping on the soggy grass. "How did that happen?"

I gulped. "I added a piece of cottonwood. It sent out sparks and one landed on the grass. Sorry about that."

41

"Well, next time, hose down the area before we have a campfire. Aunt Sara would be very unhappy if we burned down her cabin."

"Right."

"Where's Robbyn?" Dad asked, scanning the area.

Her teddy bear lay on the porch step where she'd been sitting. But she was nowhere in sight.

"Robbyn!" Dad called, turning in circles. "Where are you honey? The fire's all out. It's safe now." He strode into the cabin still calling her name. When he came out, he had two flashlights. "She's not inside. Where could she have run off to?" He handed one flashlight to me. "I'll look up the drive, you check the outhouse."

"OK."

But she wasn't there, either.

My heart thudded in my chest as I searched the darkness for any movement. How far could a little girl go in a few minutes? The smoke would have made it hard to see where she was going. That dang smoke! It seemed to have a life of its own, like it wanted to hurt us somehow.

Dad kept marching up toward the road calling Robbyn's name.

I headed the other way, down the footpath toward the river. I wanted to run but I kept my pace slow, sweeping the areas in front of me and on both sides with my light. After about fifty paces, the beam landed on a pale lump in the middle of the path. She was sprawled out on the ground, not moving. I knelt down and touched her back. She was breathing.

"Robbyn. It's me. Zeke."

Her arm moved, then her head. I rolled her over and her eyes fluttered open.

"I saw him," she whispered.

"Who?"

"The smoke person. He picked me up."

I was having trouble processing this. A puff of smoke could not pick up a forty-five pound girl. She must have panicked and run away when the grass caught fire. Maybe she tripped and hit her head. I ran my hand over her face and hair, brushing away pieces of dirt.

"Did you fall? Are you hurt?"

"No. He carried me." She raised her arms over her head. "Like this."

Robbyn always had a vivid imagination, but this was too much. I had to let Dad know she was OK. I got her to her feet and she seemed steady. Holding hands, we headed back to the cabin.

"Dad! I found her. She's all right!"

He came loping back down the drive and scooped her up in his arms.

"Oh, baby. You had us so worried!"

She nuzzled her head into his neck. "I love you, Daddy."

"Love you, too, Sweetheart."

As the two of them entered the warm glow of the cabin, I stared at the fire pit. The cursed black log sat like a slug in the middle of the dying coals, hissing and sending out steam. I grabbed the hose, still gushing water, and shot it at the miserable log until the whole fire pit was a soggy black mess. So much for that experiment.

CHAPTER 8

It took me a long time to fall asleep that night. I kept going over what happened to Robbyn and her saying the smoke person had carried her off. When she was four she had an imaginary friend called Lisa Lollypop. Dad and I played along with her whenever she talked about having a tea party with Lisa or making presents for her. We both agreed this was her way of dealing with Mom's death two years before. Mom had cancer and by the time she found out about it, she was too far gone. Too late for chemo. Her passing hit Dad and me hardest. Robbyn was so young, she didn't understand why Mom was gone. Lisa Lollypop became her substitute mother.

So was the smoke person just another imaginary friend? He sure didn't bring comfort to any of us. Just the opposite. If he wasn't imaginary, was he a ghost? Every time that old wood was burned, something weird happened. Did burning it release the ghost? I shuddered to think whose ghost it might be. The boy's ghost? But what did he want? Why was he trying to hurt Robbyn? Ideas and questions rolled around in my head until I drifted off into a fitful sleep.

I woke with a headache from a crazy dream, feeling all sick and achy, like I'd been running in my sleep. I tried to shake it off and forget about it. None of it ever happened. It wasn't real. But some parts of the dream seemed all too real—this cabin, the river, looking down from the tall cottonwood trees.

My head cleared when I caught the sweet aroma of hotcakes and syrup. Dad and Robbyn were already at the table when I stumbled out.

"Look who's up!" greeted Dad. "You looked dead to the world so we decided to let you sleep in."

"He jiggled the bed all night," complained Robbyn. She drizzled more syrup over her pancakes until they sat in a brown puddle.

I poured myself some juice. "Sorry, kid. I had bad dreams or something."

"The bed jiggled like pudding," said Robbyn.

Dad set a steaming stack of hotcakes on my plate. "What are your plans for the day?"

"I don't know. Maybe take that old bike out for a ride?"

"Where to?"

"Can I ride up to the store at Rustic?"

Dad thought a moment. "You'll have to go on the highway to get there."

"I'll be careful."

"We're at a higher altitude here," he said, pouring batter on the griddle for more pancakes. "Take it easy. I'm sure what happened to Robbyn last night was a bit of altitude sickness."

I didn't buy that for a second.

"Bring me some candy," asked Robbyn, her chin splotched with syrup.

I handed her a napkin. "Like you need any more sweets." Robbyn's birthday was in a few days so going up to the store would be a chance to get her a present without her hanging around.

Dad followed me out to the garage and I showed him the bike. The tires still looked good. He gave my shoulder a fatherly squeeze. "Don't be gone too long. I'm counting on you to keep an eye on Robbyn as much as possible. I've got to make some progress on my book. Haven't had much chance to write since we arrived and I'm way behind."

After a squirt of oil on the bike's gears, I hopped on and pedaled up the driveway to the road. It was a clear day with plump white clouds floating in an intense blue sky. A steady breeze kept it from being too hot but I soon worked up a sweat pumping uphill to Rustic.

A plan had formed in my mind sometime during the night. It kinda freaked me out at first, but as I played with the idea, I knew I had to try it. If Fred had lived in Rustic all his life, then he knew everyone here, and their stories. He said he and the boy were friends but I bet there was a lot more to it. If the dead boy's ghost was haunting us, there had to be a good reason.

I'd read somewhere that ghosts, if they really existed, were spirits of people who had unfinished business when they died. They came back to find answers or settle scores so they can pass on to whatever stage was next. But what 'score' would a boy have? He'd hardly lived his life. I had to find out more about him before more weird stuff happened, especially to Robbyn. She could be a pain sometimes, but she was my little sister and I had a job to do as her big brother.

The cabins at Rustic Resort nestled between pines along the river's edge behind the store. It was easy to spot which one was Fred's. For one thing, he was right out front working on his old pickup, banging away at something under the hood.

"Hey," I said, raising my voice.

He turned, looking at me like I was interrupting something really important. "What do you want? Horses out again?"

"No. I wanted to ask you something."

He stood up and wiped his greasy hands on a rag from his pocket. His eyes narrowed. "What about?"

"You said you were friends with the boy who died in the tree. What was his name?"

"Joey. Joey Sullivan."

"How old was he?"

"Ten."

"Did he have any brothers or sisters? Any family trouble?"

Fred rubbed his brow leaving a smudge. "I can't see how a boy who died fifty years ago is any of your business."

I listened to the quiet ripples of the river, trying to think of a way to explain. "It's just that some strange things have happened at the cabin. Things I think are connected to Joey."

"Like what?"

I hesitated. Now I was on the spot. Would he think I was nuts to talk about a ghost in pieces of wood? If I didn't ask, I'd never get answers, so I plunged in.

"We've been using some old wood from a wood pile in the garage. Aunt Sara said the wood came from the lightning-struck tree. But every time we burn a piece, some weird smoke comes out and it takes the shape of a person, or a ghost. Last night, my sister Robbyn claims it carried her off and dumped her on the ground."

Fred chuckled, crossed his arms and shook his head. "Yer nuts."

"But what if it's Joey's ghost? What if he's trying to tell us something?"

"Ain't nothin' to tell. Now leave me alone. I got work to do." With that, he ducked back under the hood of his truck. Discussion over.

My head still full of questions, I walked back toward the store. It was clear Fred didn't want to be bothered. At least I now knew the boy's name and age. He was just a couple of years younger than me.

A bell jangled over the door as I stepped into the store. Anabelle was stocking shelves and Vern was showing a fisherman a couple of lures.

"Now this here beauty works wonders with trout," explained Vern, giving me a nod as I passed.

"A Wooly Bugger," said the fisherman. "Good. I'll take three."

I cruised the candy aisle, picking out Robbyn's favorites, some cashews for Dad and sunflower seeds for myself. The other shelves had coffee mugs, T-shirts, travel books, and other tourist junk. Nothing Robbyn would like. I glanced up. A large wooden bear carved from pine was straddling one of the rafters looking down at me. Too bad he was so big. Robbyn would love a carved bear.

Anabelle spotted me and came over. "Hello again. Stocking up?"

I smiled. "All the basic food groups. Got any apples?"

"Sure." She pointed to a box at the end of the counter. "New crop, just came in."

"For the horses," I said, adding three to my pile on the counter. "I made friends with one of them yesterday." As she weighed the apples I added, "Fred got our fence fixed. No more loose horses now."

She nodded. "Good. He knows how to fix everything."

"He's sure hard to talk to. Aunt Sara told me about a boy was killed years ago when a tree was hit by lightning. I tried asking him about it and he about bit my head off."

Anabelle sighed and her shoulders slumped. "Oh yes, that was his friend, Joey. They were best friends as kids. Never saw the two of them apart. We were quite a gang back in those days. Fred and Joey, Vern and me. Plus a few other kids from up the canyon."

"Fred must have been pretty upset when Joey died."

"He changed after that happened. He went from being a happy-go-lucky boy to being quiet and moody." Anabelle glanced nervously across the store where Vern was still discussing lures with the fisherman. "I probably shouldn't be telling you all this. Fred's a real private person."

"Was he there when it happened?"

"He said he wasn't, that it was just a freak accident. I often wondered if he saw it happen and that's what made him change."

"What about Joey's parents?"

"They were hit hard by his death. Joey was their only child. Tall for his age, but a bit slow in his thinking. His parents moved away soon after it happened."

She rang up my purchases and put them in a plastic bag. "You're awfully interested in something that happened so long ago."

I shrugged. "I'm just curious is all." I turned and pointed to up the carved bear. "Do you have any small bears like that?"

She shook her head. "Used to, but we're all sold out. We get them from the artist across the street, John Begay. I'm sure he'd have some smaller ones."

I thanked her and headed for the door.

CHAPTER 9

Across the street stood a huge two-story log building that looked at least a hundred years old. Elk antlers sprouted between the second story windows and a wild collection of carved wooden animals lined the porch in front. Mostly bears, but also deer, rabbits, sheep and one of a rugged Indian in full headdress. Over the porch an old sign, Thunderhead Lodge—1898, creaked in the breeze.

A smaller wood sign on the front door said "Come on in" so I did. Inside it was dark and cool and smelled like fresh cut pine. A huge Navajo rug hung on the wall and smaller ones covered the floor. Over by the stone fireplace a man leaned over a length of pine log braced with a vise. He was intent on chipping away small bits of wood. Chips of shaved wood curled at his feet.

"Hello?" I said, stepping into his lighted area.

The man raised a hand, acknowledging me, then gave the wood one more swipe with his knife. "Have a seat." He gestured toward a chair made from the trunk of a tree.

I sat, surprised how comfortable it was.

He continued to carve, his dark weathered face serious with concentration. He wore his thick black hair gathered with red yarn at his neck. On his wrist gleamed a silver and turquoise bracelet.

"It always takes me a while to get started on a new project," he said. "I have to wait and see what the wood is telling me. Then I will know what animal is captured inside so I can set it free."

"What's that going to be?" I asked.

He paused, stroking the wood. "A fox. A silky red fox." He pointed to a spot where the wood curved. "See? Here is his tail."

"You do nice work."

"It keeps me outta trouble."

"I was hoping you had a small carved bear. My little sister loves bears and it's her birthday soon."

He put down his knife and smiled. "Bears are my favorite animal to carve." He waved his arm across the room. "Look over on that shelf by the window."

He had bears all right. Dozens of them. Sleeping bears, bears on all fours, bears on two legs, curled up, stretched out, and waving hello. I picked up one of the waving bears. "She'd love this one. How much?"

"That one is seventy-five."

"Dollars?"

"That's right."

I put it back on the shelf. "Um, I'll have to ask my dad. I don't have that much with me right now."

"Are you here for a while? I could hold it for you."

"We're staying at my Aunt Sara's cabin down the road. For a year probably, Dad says."

A broad grin spread across his face. "You folks are my neighbors then. And you'll need firewood for the winter. I have piles of leftover wood out back. I can give your father a good price."

The mention of firewood got me thinking. Here was a man who knew all about wood. He might have answers for me. "You said the wood tells you what animal is inside before you carve. How does that work?"

"As I work, I sense the spirit of the animal."

"Could there be a human spirit inside the wood?"

He wiped his big hands on his jeans. "That depends on the wood."

"What about wood that had been hit by lightning?"

His brow wrinkled as he shook his head. "Then I'd leave it alone. Native people say that disturbing wood that has been hit by lightning could make bad things happen. Maybe even release bad spirits."

Worry crept up my back like a spider. I'd already messed with the old cottonwood and released a bad spirit. I started to pace, my fears growing. "Oh, man. What if the spirit is already out? What would you do?"

He looked at me, his eyes narrowed. "If the spirit is bothering you, you need to find out what it wants. But that could be dangerous."

"How dangerous?"

"If the spirit is very angry, it might cause great pain or even death. You may need to call in a shaman or get some protection."

"Protection?"

He went over to his desk and lifted up a brown beaded necklace. He rubbed the small beads between his fingers then placed it around my neck. "This is made of juniper seeds. Some people call them Ghost Beads. Keep this on to protect you from the evil spirits."

"Do you believe in ghosts?"

"I try to keep an open mind."

I thanked him and tucked the necklace under my shirt. His warning scared me a little but as I biked back to the cabin, I decided the best way to keep away from evil spirits was to never touch that old wood again.

CHAPTER 10

It was easy to stay away from evil spirits for a while. Dad had me scraping and sanding the logs on the cabin's outer walls, getting them ready for a fresh coat of paint. While I scraped, he kept busy mixing up his own brew of sealant for the wooden porch and steps. I liked painting. It's the prep I couldn't stand. My hands were sore and my knuckles full of scratches when he finally said we'd be making the one-hour trip into town to do some shopping.

We stocked up again on groceries since the little store at Rustic only had the bare essentials and their prices were high. At Home Depot Dad bought paint, brushes, turpentine, nails and rolls of insulation for the attic. Robbyn asked for a six-pack of flowers to plant by the steps.

"Good idea," said Dad, handing her the plastic bag holding the flowers. "A woman's touch will add some beauty to the place."

She liked that, being called 'a woman.'

Driving back up the canyon, I tried to find out where Dad stood on the subject of ghosts. I had to ask him carefully or he'd think I was crazy. "After Mom died, did you ever sense her spirit around you?"

He glanced over at me. "Why do you ask?"

I shrugged, as if it weren't important. "I was talking to the wood carver in Rustic. He says he can feel the spirit in the wood he carves. I just wondered if spirits appear in other places."

He nodded. "I did sense her once, soon after she passed. It was just a feeling that she was nearby, checking on us. It made me feel good."

"So you didn't actually see her, like a ghost?"

"Oh no. Nothing like that."

"I saw a ghost," piped up Robbyn from the back seat. "It was the smoke person."

Dad gave me a warning look. "Now sweetie, don't let Zeke get you seeing things. There's no such thing as ghosts. What I was saying about your mother was just a feeling of peace. Nothing spooky."

I let the subject drop. It was clear Dad didn't want me saying things that would scare Robbyn. But his comment about a peaceful spirit did make me feel better. I wished Mom's spirit would visit me sometime.

By the time we got back to the cabin, an afternoon storm had churned up, bringing wind and rain. Our work on the outside was put on hold for a while. Dad set Robbyn up at the table with her flowers, a bag of potting soil and six pots.

"Fill the pots half way with soil, then put in the flowers," he told her.

"I know, Daddy. We did this in kindergarten."

He beckoned to me. "Let's see what the attic has, Zeke." He dragged a stepladder into the bedroom then pointed to an access hole in the closet. "I've taken measurements up there but it'll take the two of us to get the insulation rolls in place. Plus, there's stuff that needs to come out first. You can help with that." He handed me a face mask. "Put this on first. It's a mess up there."

I climbed the stepladder and pushed aside the panel. I winced as dried bugs and sawdust fell all over my face. I wiggled up through the hole and into the small room under the roof. It wasn't so much an attic as a crawl space. The roof came slanting down sharply leaving only a few square feet of storage space. An old carpet covered the wood floor and layers of dust coated the junk stored up there. The air was stuffy and thick, not at all like the cool breezy air outside the cabin. The mask I wore made it even harder to breathe. I wanted to get this job done quickly.

I brushed away the cobwebs and started handing the stuff down to Dad through the hole. Old cane fishing rods, a broken chair, some empty picture frames, a ratty old sleeping bag, a bundle of old clothes and a box of puzzles and toys. I rolled up the carpet last, mouse droppings and all, and lowered it through the hole.

Turning around to check if I'd forgotten anything, I felt the air in the attic shift from suffocating warmth to damp and cold. How could that be? There weren't any windows to let in a cool breeze, no reason for the sudden change. I rubbed my arms and stepped toward the hole to climb down. Trouble was, I couldn't see the hole any more. Inky shadows from the corners loomed larger, closing in on me. A gray fog crept across the floor, undulating like a giant snake. It wrapped around my ankle and made me fall with a thud.

"You OK up there?" asked Dad from below.

At the sound of his voice, the mysterious fog disappeared and the shadows receded. I scrabbled my way toward the hole and looked down. "Yeah, I—I just stumbled." With one last nervous glance around the attic to see who or what had grabbed me, I slipped through the hole and onto the stepladder. In the daylight and safety of the bedroom I decided that my imagination was playing tricks on me up there. I'd probably stirred up a cloud of dust and caught my pant leg on a nail sticking out, nothing more. And I kept telling myself that because nothing else made sense.

Dad and I hauled the carpet outside. No way were we going to keep that messy rag inside. Same with the grungy sleeping bag. It was filthy, full of stains and holes, and when I unrolled it, a dead mouse.

I brought the box of toys out to the main room for Robbyn to sort through. Putting her flower planting project aside, she reached for the box. She pulled out a catcher's mitt, a baseball, a bag of plastic cowboys and Indians, and a dump truck.

"Nothing fun for me," she said. "Except maybe this." She lifted out a box of colored chalk. But her smile faded when she realized we had no concrete driveway and no sidewalk to draw on.

"You could draw faces on your rock people," I suggested.

"I could draw on my pots!" She picked up a clay pot and started to color yellow zig-zags around the edge.

I picked up the mitt and baseball. The mitt was about the same size as my own. Who had played with it? For a moment, I wished my ex-friend Taylor was here so we could play catch. My life back in Phoenix seemed so far away and long ago. Our stupid argument was just that—stupid.

"What's this?" From the bottom of the box I pulled out a thick photo album. I sat down at the table and started turning the pages. There were faded color photos of kids out in a field shooting a rifle at a target, adults barbecuing chicken, families posing around a birthday cake, winter scenes of kids bundled up and skating on a frozen lake. The cabin looked different, taken years ago when the trees were smaller. In one picture, two

61

little boys leaned on a hand pump, probably what they used before the electric pump was installed.

Then one photo jumped out at me. I stared at it, feeling the hairs on my arms stand up. It was a shot of two boys waving from a tree fort built high up in a tree. It was an odd tree, shaped like a V or a Y, but perfect for supporting the platform of the fort. The boys looked younger than me, wearing T-shirts and jeans, one with shaggy blond hair, the other with dark hair.

I'd bet anything one of the boys was the one who died. Who was the other boy? I pried the photo off the page and tucked it in my pocket.

CHAPTER 11

I was sitting at the table fiddling with the radio when Dad marched into the room brandishing fishing poles and wearing a goofy hat stuck with fishhooks. "Today we catch our dinner! Vern told me about a lake that's just jumping with brown trout."

"A lake? Where?"

"Up the road about five miles, then a short hike through the forest to Lake Marie. Vern says it's beautiful. I got Robbyn dressed, so you better get ready, too."

Robbyn shuffled out of the bedroom wearing long pants, a long-sleeved shirt and a floppy hat. "I'm hot in all these clothes," she whined. "Can't I wear my shorts?"

Dad called her over. "Nope." He grabbed a can of bug spray from the counter. "Here, let me put some repellant on you. There may be skeeters on the trail and I bet you don't want them to make lunch out of you."

"I'll do my own bug spray," I said, reaching for the can. I didn't want Dad poking around my shirt and finding the ghost beads.

He tossed the can to me. "While you get ready, I'll make up some sandwiches for our lunch."

Actually, some time away from the cabin sounded like a good idea. I fingered the beads I'd tucked under my shirt. Ever since my talk with Mr. Begay, I'd been worrying about what bad things the ghost from the wood might do. I needed a break and some time to think of how to handle things if he came back.

A half-hour later Dad parked the car at a pullout near the mile marker Vern had told him about. Dense trees crowded the road on both sides. I didn't see any sign of a lake.

"How far is this place?" I asked.

"About a mile. Up that way." He pointed off into the woods where a thin trail cut through the underbrush. He handed me a backpack with our lunch inside. "You take this. I'll carry the fishing gear."

"And I'll carry Bear," said Robbyn. "He'll scare off the real bears."

"Like me!" I roared and chased after her.

"Nooooo!"

"Knock it off, Zeke," said Dad.

"Just testing to see how brave she is."

Robbyn stuck out her tongue at me.

Following the trail meant climbing over small boulders at times and wading across puny streams that dribbled through the brush. Dad went first, Robbyn in the middle, and I stayed behind her to make sure she didn't wander off. The first fifteen minutes of the hike Dad and I walked in silence while Robbyn chattered to her stuffed bear. Then she started complaining, her voice high and squeaky.

"How much farther?"

"Not far," said Dad.

"I'm tired."

He passed her a small candy bar. "Here's some quick energy."

She dropped the wrapper. I picked it up.

"Are we there yet?"

"Soon." Another candy bar passed to my crabby sister. "Want one Zeke?"

"No, I'm good."

"Bear needs some candy, too."

By the time we finally reached the lake, Robbyn had gobbled up all the candy bars. But at least she'd stopped grumbling about the hike.

Lake Marie sat in a bowl surrounded by rocky cliffs with gravelly slopes stretching all the way down to the water's edge. The water changed colors as it got deeper, from pale aqua to deep purple. In the middle of the lake a little tree-covered island sat all by itself. Of course, that's where Robbyn wanted to go.

"No way, Sweetie," said Dad.

"We could swim," she suggested.

"Stick your fingers in the water."

She plunged her whole hand in and yanked it out fast. "Oh! Too cold."

"Yup." He guided us to a flat grassy area where she wouldn't risk falling in like she had at the river.

Hooks loaded with bait, lines drooping in the water, we sat quietly waiting for a bite. And wouldn't you know, the first one to get a tug was Robbyn. After all her yammering about coming up here, she got the first fish.

We had lunch and caught four more fish. Then it was time to head back. Dad challenged Robbyn and me to a game of spotting wildlife on the way, which made the hike back to the car go much faster. Robbyn called out three rabbits and countless birds. But I scored the biggest hit. A moose wearing a huge rack of antlers went crashing through the brush. Dad saw him, too, but let me get the spotting.

On the drive back to the cabin, Robbyn dozed in the back seat, her teddy bear tucked under her chin.

We were driving along, just talking about family stuff when this boy appeared from nowhere, standing in the middle of the road. He didn't move or even look startled as our van barreled toward him.

I yelled, "Look out!"

Dad slammed on the brakes and swerved, sending the van skidding into a rocky ditch. Robbyn screamed as she slid with a thud onto the back floor. I sat frozen, arms braced against the dashboard, listening to my own thundering heartbeat.

"You kids all right?" asked Dad, rubbing his forehead.

I glanced back at Robbyn who was climbing up from the floor. She looked a little dazed. "Yeah, we're good," I said.

Where had that kid in the road come from? Did we hit him? Teeth gritted, I jumped out, dreading what I might see on the pavement. But the boy wasn't there. Dad climbed slowly out of the van, a bloody cut oozing on his forehead.

"Stupid deer!"

"A deer? No, it was a boy." I turned in a circle, wondering if we'd hit him so hard he'd landed in the bushes. Dad trotted over to check one side of the road, I scanned the other. No child. Not even a drop of blood on the pavement or a shred of clothing.

"It was definitely a deer," said Dad, dabbing his wound with a handkerchief. "He jumped right in front of the van."

I stared at him. Had he hit his head so hard, he'd gotten mixed up? That was no deer on the road. It was a boy wearing a striped shirt and blue jeans. He didn't look anything like a deer.

"It was a boy. I'm sure of it."

"Then where is he?"

We both stood in the middle of the road, eyes peeled, looking for a boy who wasn't there. A boy who'd looked vaguely familiar but then had totally vanished. Like a ghost.

"Daddy!"

He loped back to her. "You all right, Toots?"

"I think so. What happened?"

"I swerved to avoid hitting a deer. We'll be back on the road soon."

Dad was completely wrong about the deer but I wasn't going to argue. Whatever it was, we were now in a ditch. And when I saw the result, I groaned.

"Bad news, Dad," I said. "We're not going anywhere. Two tires are blown."

CHAPTER 12

"Tow truck will be here in a few," said Vern, running his hand through his shaggy gray hair.

"Then what?" asked Dad.

"You'll ride along with the tow truck guy down the river. They have the tires you need at the Shell station in town. You'll be good as new in a few hours."

Our accident had happened just a mile from Rustic so after a short hike up the road we were there. I was sure happy to see that funky old place. Anabelle made a fuss over Robbyn and me and quickly patched up Dad's forehead with ointment and a bandage. Vern called for the tow truck.

Robbyn sat moaning on a bench, holding her stomach. "I don't feel so good," she whimpered.

"Too many candy bars and too much excitement," said Dad. Then, turning to Anabelle, "Is it all right if the kids stay here with you while I take care of the van?"

Anabelle grinned. "Of course, no problem. I could use the company."

Dad handed over his fishing basket. "If I'm not back by suppertime..."

Vern peeked inside. "I know just what to do with these beauties! Come on, Zeke. I'll show you how to clean them."

I followed Vern out to the edge of the river. With one flick of a knife blade, he 'unzipped' the belly of the fish and dumped the contents into the river.

"Snacks for other fish," he explained.

Fish guts didn't sit well with me. My stomach lurched and I had to hold on not to barf into the river. My head ached, too.

"Now I feel woozy." I placed my hand on my forehead.

"You got a touch of altitude sickness, I reckon," said Vern. He led me to a hammock slung between two pine trees. I crawled in and closed my eyes. "Rest now. I'll come and check on you in a while."

Altitude sickness. That was the second time it was blamed for someone not feeling good. Dad said it was altitude sickness that made Robbyn fall on the path. I had a feeling it was something else. I couldn't think straight. All I wanted was to sleep and to forget. But forget what? I folded my arm over my eyes and drifted into dreamland.

I was lost in a dark forest, searching for something. My friend Taylor stepped out from behind a tree, asking me to come play ball. But

THE GHOST IN THE WOOD

when I looked at him again, all I saw was a big box. Then I was inside as it tumbled down a steep hill down, down, down into a rushing river. Water filled the box and fish swam up to my face. They looked at me with their bulging eyes, their little mouths opening and closing, bubbles all around. One fish face became a boy, his fish body made of red and blue stripes. He opened his mouth and the water turned red, red, red.

I woke up gasping, flailing my arms in the air, rocking the hammock until it twisted and dumped me on the ground. With that jolt it hit me where I'd seen the boy on the road before—in that old photo album we'd found in the attic. Even though I only saw him for an instant, I knew it was the same boy on the road. Same face, same jeans, same striped shirt. He was a ghost now and he was following us, trying to hurt us. But why?

It was late when Dad got back. Robbyn was feeling better but she looked pale and droopy.

"She threw up a couple of times," said Anabelle. "I gave her something to calm her stomach. She's dehydrated from the sickness so be sure she gets extra fluids in her. She'll be better in the morning."

Dad carried Robbyn out to the van and when we got back to the cabin, he carried her in to bed. No happy chatter, no request for a bedtime story from my little sister.

After stoking the potbellied stove with wood—pine, not the old cottonwood—we sat at the table in silence for a while. Dad leaned forward and massaged his temples. He didn't look so hot. He had bags under his eyes and his whole face sagged like a basset hound's. The woozy feeling I'd felt earlier was gone, but now it was replaced with dread, a fear that I'd brought all this on by stirring up a ghost.

"It's times like this I really miss your mother, Zeke. She had the touch. She knew how to make things better. I don't know what to do when you kids get sick and if I do try something, I don't know if it's the right thing."

"It's not your fault, Dad. Robbyn will be fine."

"I hope you're right. This parenting job is harder than I ever imagined. Thanks for all you do to help. Don't know what I'd do without you." He got up and headed for his bedroom. "What a day. A long hike, an accident, tow ride into town and back. No wonder I'm beat. See you in the morning."

Guilt washed over me. If I hadn't messed with that wood, we wouldn't have had so much trouble. As I crawled into my bunk, I peeked down at Robbyn. Her arm was tucked around her teddy bear and she was sleeping quietly. I hoped she'd be better in the morning. I couldn't shake the idea that we were being haunted by a ghost. Too many things had happened to us and it had to stop. My plan for tomorrow was to get some answers.

CHAPTER 13

Robbyn was not better in the morning. In fact, she was worse. She had a fever, her face was all splotchy red and her hair stringy with sweat. She didn't want to eat or get up. Dad was in a panic. He called Anabelle and she came over with a thermos of chicken soup. While he was distracted chatting with her, I butted in and asked if I could ride up to Rustic. He mumbled a quick, "Yeah, fine." I know I took advantage of him while he was worried about Robbyn, but I had to get out of there.

Outside, the sun felt warm and a soft breeze whispered through the pines. It was a great day but everything felt off, not quite right. Robbyn's illness was way more than too many candy bars and altitude sickness. We'd been here over a week so we must have adjusted to the altitude by now. Was it the smoke ghost causing the trouble? Being careful not to disturb the woodpile, I got the bike out of the garage and headed up the road.

The one person I could talk to about my ghost theory was Mr. Begay. His belief that spirits, both good and bad, could be locked up in a piece of wood made me sure he'd understand. No way was I going to talk to Dad about it. He had enough to worry about. He wouldn't know what to do anyway.

I found Mr. Begay in the back of his studio working a fire inside what looked like a little stone hut with a round roof. A bed of hot coals glowed underneath the dome and a soft white smoke rose from the chimney.

"What's that?" I asked.

Mr. Begay tapped the dome with a stick. "It's an oven. I bake bread for the café across the street, plus the occasional pizza."

"Cool. Do you do take-out?"

"Just let me know what you want on it." He motioned me over to a bench under the trees. "What can I do for you, besides pizza? Still interested in that bear?"

"No. I came about something else. I'm hoping you can help me." I pulled the juniper berry necklace out from my shirt. "I don't think these ghost beads are working."

"What's happened?"

"Since you gave them to me, we had an accident when Dad swerved to avoid hitting something. Dad claims a deer jumped in front of the van but I saw a boy standing in the road. But when we got out to investigate, there was nothing there. No boy and no deer. And when I was clearing out the attic in our cabin something grabbed my ankle and made me fall. But no one was there. Now my sister is real sick."

"Interesting." He folded his arms and looked to the sky. "It sounds like you're being tormented by a Chindi—a ghost who is trying to get your attention. I had a cousin who was made ill by the ghost sickness. He had taken some clothes that belonged to his brother who died. He got so weak he spent a month in bed. The Chindi finally left him when he had his wife burn the clothes he had stolen. Have you been in contact with anything connected to a dead person?"

"Yes. I think so." I shoved my hands deep into my pockets. "When I was here the last time, I asked you about lightning-struck wood."

"I said it should be avoided."

"Well, I didn't know that. I found some old wood in the garage by our cabin. As soon as I touched it, weird things started to happen. The first night here we burned some in the stove and a smoke ghost appeared. Of course Dad thought it was plain old smoke, but later that night it tried to get in my room. Then another night I burned more wood and the smoke ghost carried off my little sister and left her on the dirt."

"Do you know who this ghost is?"

"I think it's the ghost of a boy named Joey who was killed when a tree was hit by lightning a long time ago. He and his friend had a tree fort by the river."

"I see. Disturbing the wood has released him. Spirits who don't pass on to the next world often stay in this world because they have unfinished business. Some are looking for revenge. Some want answers. Some just want to move on. You need to find out what this ghost wants. Only then will he be able to rest."

"How do I find out what he wants? Do I burn more wood to make him appear? I don't want my dad or my sister hurt."

Mr. Begay got up and stirred the fire under the oven. "Bring a piece of wood over here. We will burn it together. You should not face this ghost alone."

"What if he won't appear with you around?"

"We'll see. If he's truly anxious to solve something in this world and move on, he will come."

"When should we do this?"

"Can you come back up here tonight at ten? It should be totally dark by then. Ghosts like the dark so let's keep him happy."

I squirmed on the bench, thinking. "It might be hard. I'd have to sneak out without waking Dad. But, yeah. I'll be here."

"Good. Meet me here by the oven. If he doesn't show, we'll make some pizza."

On the way back to the cabin I considered telling Dad. But in the end, I decided against it. He would just say no and keep me home. I didn't like sneaking out, but to save Robbyn from any more sickness, it had to be done.

CHAPTER 14

Sneaking out was harder than I thought. It was almost ten and Dad was still up working on his book. Every fifteen minutes he'd get up and peek into our bedroom to check on Robbyn. Her fever was down and she'd eaten some of Anabelle's soup for dinner. Her quiet snores told me she was sleeping soundly. But Dad was still nervous about her.

Finally, the lights in the main room went out and I heard him shuffle off to bed. I checked my watch. 10:05. I hoped Mr. Begay hadn't given up on me. It would take another fifteen minutes for me to bike up to his place. I slid down from my bunk as quietly as I could but Robbyn woke when I picked up my backpack.

"Where are you going?" she asked, rubbing her eyes.

"Outhouse. Go back to sleep."

"Don't be gone for long. It's spooky in here without you."

"Shh. Don't wake Dad."

She lay back on her pillow and hugged her bear. I waited until I saw her eyes close again then I slipped out the door. If Dad came out to see what I was doing, I would use the same excuse about the outhouse. But he didn't come. I ducked into the garage, gulped down my fears, and stashed a piece of the wood in my backpack. Soon I was heading up our drive toward the highway.

An almost full moon cast an eerie light making long shadows dance along my way. No cars or trucks zoomed along the road at this hour but it wasn't totally quiet. Off in the woods a coyote howled and an owl hoo-hooed from a power pole. I pedaled harder, trying not to think about the ghost-wood I was carrying on my back.

Mr. Begay was there, fanning the coals of his bread oven.

"I thought you'd changed your mind," he said when I wheeled my bike into his yard.

"Dad stayed up late. Thanks for waiting." I slung my backpack on the ground and pulled out the chunk of wood. It was charred black on the outside like the other pieces.

Mr. Begay examined it, turning the wood over in his big hands. "You say this came from a tree that was hit many years ago?"

"Yes. Anabelle said it happened about fifty years ago."

He shook his head as he thumped the log with his knuckles, listening to the sound. "Cottonwood is soft and rots easily. For this piece to still be around after fifty years, it must have special powers."

"Yeah, like ghost powers."

"Very possible. Let's find out."

He leaned down and tossed the chunk of wood into the hot coals. The smoke from the chimney turned from pale gray to dark gray. It swirled up like a fat ribbon, curling through the night air, up, up into the trees. I expected the smoke to come down and cover us but it just kept going, blocking out the moon and hiding the stars with a thin haze. Maybe that's what made the night suddenly feel much colder. Goosebumps prickled my arms and back. I turned to ask Mr. Begay what he thought but he was just sitting there, not looking up, not reacting. Like in a trance. And standing right behind him was the boy.

He looked so normal, like a lost little kid. Shaggy blond hair, a red and white striped shirt, jeans with ragged holes in the knees. No shoes. I could almost believe he was a real boy except for the golden aura that surrounded him like a halo.

"Are you Joey?" I asked.

He nodded.

"Why are you here?"

He pointed to the oven.

"Because we burned the wood?"

He nodded again.

"Can't you talk?"

He shook his head.

I sighed. How was I going to find out what he wanted if he couldn't talk? My only chance was to ask him yes-no questions.

"Are you a ghost because of the lightning bolt?"

He nodded.

I wanted to know why he hadn't come down from the tree, who was with him, what was he doing up there in a storm. All questions that couldn't be answered with yes or no. "Do you want to move on?"

He smiled this time. A sad smile.

This was so frustrating. And weird. Here I was talking to a kid who died fifty years ago. Who would believe me? "How can I help you?"

He pointed to his mouth and then to me.

"Should I tell someone?"

He turned and pointed across the road to Rustic Resort.

"Tell Anabelle?"

He shook his head.

"Tell Vern? Fred?"

He kept shaking his head. The aura around him pulsed orange with anger. He shook his fists then made climbing moves with his feet and arms.

"You climbed up the tree?"

His head bobbed briskly.

"But you didn't come down when the storm hit."

He swayed and covered his ears like you do when thunder booms. Then he waved his arms across his body, like the wind was blowing hard.

"The wind blew something?"

He made climbing motions, then a shoving move.

"I get it! The wind blew something down!"

He whirled around and pointed across the road.

"Fred did something?"

Slowly, he faced me again, his eyes full of fire. He had changed from a sad little boy to something wild, something out of control. My stomach tightened and my heart thumped harder.

"But what do you want? To get even?"

His face contorted as he kicked and punched an invisible enemy coming at me with a fury I'd never seen before until I crouched down on my knees, shielding my head with my arms to ward off his blows. The air thickened into a dense and suffocating fog making me choke and gasp for breath. Then with a sucking swish, he was gone leaving behind shadows and dust.

I unfolded my body and stared over at Mr. Begay. He hadn't moved an inch all the time Joey was with me. Now he exhaled, as if coming back to life. He blinked, rubbed his hands on his thighs and said, "Your ghost didn't come."

"Yes he did. Didn't you see him? He was right behind you!"

He glanced over his shoulder. "No. I saw nothing. I was waiting for something to happen. It's only been a few moments since we put the wood in the oven."

"Noooo. It's been a lot longer. You were out of it, locked in some sort of trance. He must not have wanted you to see him or talk to him. Just me."

Mr. Begay massaged his neck, twisting his head right and left. "That must be why I feel so stiff. What did you learn?"

"Joey's one angry ghost! I think he wants revenge for something Fred did the night of the storm. I have to warn him."

"I hope he believes you."

CHAPTER 15

It was almost midnight when I got back to the cabin. The lights were on so I knew I'd have to face Dad. He was sitting at the table, his arms folded across his chest.

"Sit down, Zeke," he said when I came in.

I sat.

"What's the big idea sneaking off like that? I was about to call the sheriff."

"I'm sorry, Dad, but if I'd asked your permission, you wouldn't have let me go."

"That's not the point. Where were you?"

"I went up to see the woodcarver, Mr. Begay."

"And this trip couldn't wait until morning because...?"

I couldn't think of any reason on earth to be biking up the road to Rustic in the dark except the truth. "I think some of the weird stuff that's happened to us lately is because of a ghost."

"A ghost?" He shook his head as if weighing the stupidity of my excuse.

"Years ago a boy was killed when lightning hit a tree. We started having problems when we burned some of the wood from that tree and the cabin filled with smoke."

"That was just the flue being clogged."

"But it wasn't, was it? What about when I found Robbyn knocked out on the path? Our accident? Robbyn's illness? Mr. Begay says the ghost was released from the wood and is trying to get our attention."

Dad chuckled. "Well, he sure got yours!"

My face got warm with embarrassment. "Anyway, Mr. Begay suggested we call out the ghost to see what he wants. That's what I was doing up at his place."

"With all due respect to Native American culture, I think that's a lot of hooey. There's no such thing as ghosts. No scientific reason for them. He's just playing into your imagination, though I can't understand why you'd fall for it."

"It's not my imagination, Dad! I saw the boy tonight. I talked to him."

Dad leaned back in his chair and sighed. "Zeke, if I didn't know any better, I'd think you were on drugs."

"I'm not into drugs. I'm as sane and clear-headed as ever." I could see disappointment in

Dad's eyes. Somehow, I'd let him down even by telling him the truth. "Honest, Dad. No drugs."

Dad heaved himself up with a sigh and ran his fingers through his hair. "I'm going back to bed. We'll talk about this more in the morning after we're both rested."

That was fine with me. As I climbed up to my bunk, Robbyn whispered in the dark, "I had to tell Daddy."

"I know. It's OK."

"I saw you ride away on your bike. I was worried."

"Thanks, Robbie. I'm all right."

My legs ached from the bike ride up and back and I wanted to sleep. But my brain was wired, replaying my contact with Joey. He'd seemed so real, so much like a normal kid, until he got angry, of course. How was I going to help him pass on to whatever's next for him? What is next? Trying to figure that out made my head hurt and I just wanted to shut down.

A pine branch scritch-scratched on our bedroom window as the wind moaned like a lost soul in the dark night. Something thumped outside but I was too tired to find out what it was. *Relax,* I told myself. *Everything is all right.* But I was wrong.

The first clue was when Dad went out on the porch to fill the water kettle in the morning. The spigot coughed out a few dribbles and then nothing.

"That's odd," he said, tapping the pipe.

Then we noticed the pump was silent. No working pump, no water. Dad hunkered down and checked the pump motor, poking a wrench at pipes and dials. "Looks like the framus is stuck into the widget and needs a jigiwig." He sat back on his heels and laughed.

"In other words, you don't have a clue what's wrong."

"Nope. Plumbing is way above my pay grade. Time to call a professional." He headed in to the cabin to phone.

I thought back to the thump I heard last night. It could have been a branch falling. Or one of the horses. Or Joey making just the kind of trouble that would get Fred over here to fix. And guess who Dad had called.

"He'll be here in twenty minutes," said Dad, waving me in from the porch. "Let's have some breakfast."

There was no way I could talk to Fred while Dad was around. I set up tarps and ladders for painting the outside of the cabin while Dad explained to Fred about the pump. The logs were chipped and sanded but the cracks still needed filling so I aimed the caulking gun at them. My ears stayed tuned to the conversation from the pump house, though. Finally I heard Dad surrender. "I'll leave you to it."

Fred shook his head. "This here pump is only a year old. No reason it shoulda conked out. No sir, no way."

"I'm sure you'll figure it out," said Dad, heading back into the cabin.

From the corner of my eye I watched as Fred tinkered with one tool then another.

"There are some more tools in the garage," I offered, coming over to him.

He threw down his wrench. "More tools, eh? Never have looked in there. Place is always locked up tight."

"It was, but the lock fell off."

He followed me into the musty old garage. I led him deeper inside.

"Back here, on the work bench, you'll find a bunch of tools."

He stepped carefully around the piles of junk. "Place is a museum in here. Fire hazard, too." He jerked a thumb at the pile of National Geographics on the floor.

"And lots of firewood." I tossed him a chunk of the ghost wood. It caught him by surprise and he almost dropped it. "Recognize that?"

He stared at the blackened wood in his arms, then back at me. "Why should I? It's just wood."

"Nope. It's from that old tree you and Joey used for a tree fort, the one hit by lightning."

He turned the wood over in his hand, stroking it lightly. "All that wood there, too?" He pointed to the pile under the tarp.

"Yup. That wood is haunted because Joey's spirit was trapped inside. It came out when I burned some of it."

"I told you that was a crazy idea. Why are you still harping on that?"

"Because Joey has been causing us trouble. I've even seen him, talked to him."

Fred snorted and tossed the wood chunk back on the pile. "And what does this ghost of yours have to say?"

"He told me—in his way—that something happened that night to keep him from coming down from the tree fort. He's angry. I'm pretty sure he's angry at you."

"I wasn't even there. Didn't see it happen."

From my shirt pocket I pulled out the old photo I found in the album. "Maybe this will jog your memory."

He took the photo from me and stared at it a moment. "Yeah, that's us."

I edged next to him and pointed to the ladder at the bottom of the picture. "You used that to get up and down, didn't you?"

"Sure. So what?"

"So why didn't Joey climb down when the storm hit?"

He shoved the photo back at me. "I told you, I wasn't there!" He started to leave the garage but a sudden cold wind slammed the heavy wooden doors shut. In the darkness, Fred tripped, or was shoved, and fell stumbling toward the doors.

"Get offa me!" he shouted, his feet scuffling on the floor.

"I'm not on you," I replied. "I'm still at the back of the garage."

I heard groans and oofs, as if someone was punching him. He kicked out, knocking more wood from the woodpile. Then as quickly as the doors had closed, they blew open, flooding the garage with light. Fred scrambled out toward his truck like he had ants in his pants. As he passed the pump house, it gave a thump and began purring with power. He never even looked back. He just jumped in his truck and tore up the driveway.

CHAPTER 16

Weather at the cabin changed in the blink of an eye. We woke up to a nice clear day but by mid-morning it looked like someone had stuffed the sky with gray pillows. A breeze rustled through the aspens and sent a chill down my neck as I stood in the corral. I breathed in the cool air, pungent with the smells of horse, leather and hay.

Didi adjusted the saddle on one of her horses, an old plodding mare named Rosie. The horse stood patiently while letting me run my hand down her long face, her tail swishing away flies and her eyes half closed.

Robbyn hung on a rail along the fence, her face aglow. "I'm going for a ride on Rosie. Didi's taking me."

Dad cast an eye toward the clouds and shook his head. "She's been bugging me about a ride on one of the horses since we got here. I hope the rain stays away."

"No worries, Matt," said Didi. "We'll go to the upper meadow, nice and easy."

"Thanks for doing this while I go in to town," said Dad. "I owe this errand to you, you know. I've got an interview with the school district about that science position."

Didi gave the saddle cinch one more tug. "You'll do fine!"

"And I need to pick up some party things. Robbyn's birthday is tomorrow. Can you come?"

"Wouldn't miss it!"

Robbyn grinned. "Yay! Daddy's going to make a cake with green frosting, right Daddy?"

"You bet!"

I pulled Dad over toward the van and whispered. "I need a present for Robbyn. Could you pick up some colored pens and a sketch pad? Think she'd like that?"

"She'd love it." Dad glanced up as Didi hoisted Robbyn into the saddle. "Keep an eye on your sister. I know hanging out with her isn't your favorite pastime."

"No problem, Dad. After the ride, we'll listen to a Rockies game on the radio."

"Good. I won't worry then."

As I watched him drive off, I thought I heard the first rumbles of thunder. They sounded far off so I figured we had plenty of time.

The horseback ride took us over an old bridge across the river and along a trail through a grassy meadow. Didi took it slow, riding side by side with Robbyn while I followed behind. I admired Didi's patience as Robbyn pestered her with horse questions. Grasshoppers shot up around us like popcorn until dark clouds hid the sun and the wind picked up. Soon fat raindrops splattered our faces. I could've kept on going—what cowboy gives up after a few raindrops? But Robbyn started to complain so Didi turned us around.

She pulled her horse, Noche, up next to mine and whispered, "Any more action from your ghost?"

I glanced over at Robbyn while keeping my voice low. "Yeah, and I'm worried."

"About what?"

"Robbyn. He's trying to get at me through her."

"Not while I'm around he won't."

"Then you'd better move in with us!"

She gave me a broad smile and clicked her tongue, guiding Noche back beside Robbyn.

Forty minutes later we were back at the corral and the rain was coming down in sheets. Even cowboys hate to get sopping wet. We hurried to get the saddles and tack off the horses and into the dry shed before dashing into the cabin.

Robbyn helped Didi make tuna sandwiches for lunch while I tuned in the Rockies baseball game on the radio. But following the action was a real challenge. The radio crackled with static when-ever something exciting happened.

Tulowitzki steps away from the plate, checks his bat.....two balls, one strike...Tulo swings and.........Martinez and Harvey going back, reaching, reaching....oh no!....great play by......and the score is....

I slapped the top of the radio. "Come on! Do your static during the commercials!"

"It's the cost of living up the canyon," said Didi. "We get spectacular views but we give up some of the benefits of living in town."

Thunder rumbles grew louder as the rain pelted the windows like marbles. Soon the rain turned heavy until it spilled like a waterfall off the roof.

"Don't you ever get gentle rain up here?"

She shook her head. "Not in the summertime. It's usually all or nothing. Besides, we need the moisture. Without rain I have to arrange for irrigation in the pasture and that gets expensive."

When the phone rang, I answered, glad to hear Dad's voice on the other end.

"It's pouring up here," I told him. "How's it down there?"

"That's why I'm calling. I'm all done in town. Interview went well, got groceries, but now I'm stuck on Highway 14 because of a mudslide. The rain washed piles of debris down from the burn area up in the hills. Cars are stopped on the road and we're all waiting for a crew to clear the mess."

"How long will that be?" I asked.

"Don't know. Put Didi on."

I handed the phone to her. She reassured Dad she could stay until he got here.

"Looks like you're stuck with me a bit longer," she said with a shrug.

Robbyn looked up from her lunch. "Isn't Daddy coming?"

"As soon as the road is cleared," Didi said. "These rock and mud slides happen whenever we get a big rainstorm. People are coming to open the road again. He'll be OK, honey."

"I hope so. He's bringing stuff for my—"

An ear-splitting boom of thunder cut her off followed by a crash and horse whinnies from the corral. Didi was out the door in an instant with me close behind.

One look told us what had happened. A huge branch from one of the tall cottonwoods near the corral had fallen on the shed roof and part of the fence. Spooked by the event, four of the horses had fled onto the driveway and were heading up toward the road, heads tossing wildly in the rain. Two others were trotting across the field.

Didi grabbed a couple of halters and tossed me a rope. "Zeke, see if you can coax those two back to the corral. I'll go after the others. If I can get Noche, the rest will follow."

I hustled across the muddy field, clicking my tongue like Didi had done to calm the horses. They stopped and looked back at me, rain dripping off their hides and manes. One was Rosie, the horse Robbyn had ridden earlier in the day.

"Hey girl," I called. "Come on home. Easy, easy." The horses let me get closer, perhaps remembering the apples I'd given them the day before. Thunder grumbled overhead and they startled again. But Rosie turned and trotted back to me. The other one followed. I looped the rope around Rosie's neck and grabbed the mane of the other. Slowly, we made our way back to the shed. Even though part of the roof was smashed, most of it still offered protection from the rain and wind.

Rain and wind whipped across my face. I cupped my hands to my eyes to see if I could spot Didi and the other horses. She was coming down the driveway, riding Noche and leading the other three behind her.

I tied my two horses to a rail and then took a look at the fence. The leafy part of the branch had broken the fence down but it was too heavy to move by myself. Instead, I hauled a piece of the tin roof from the shed over and propped it up to close the gap. Didi nodded approval as she and her horses plodded through my makeshift gate.

Once the horses were secured again, we dragged our soggy selves back to the cabin. But our feeling of relief evaporated when we spotted a thin trail of smoke leading from the cabin down toward the river.

"Oh no!" exclaimed Didi, rushing to the door.

There was no fire but Robbyn was gone.

CHAPTER 17

Didi quickly checked the bedrooms, then headed for the door. "She's not here. Where could she have gone?"

I put my hand out to stop her. "Wait a sec! I think I know. She's down by the river."

"Why there?"

"That smoke trail. Come on."

I tore out the door with Didi following. I sprinted down the footpath, my feet flying over rocks, weeds and bushes. Thunder and lightning exploded above us, flashing the way in pulses of black and white. The rain lashed at my face and I had to keep wiping my eyes to see where I was going. My lungs were about to burst when I reached a tree that stood like a sentinel next to the old stump. Up above, a vapor hung like a shroud in the branches. The air stank of sulfur. I couldn't see Robbyn but I could hear her crying.

"Robbyn? It's me and Didi."

"Get me down!"

"We will. Just stay still."

"Help me!"

"I will, I will. But we have to get help."

"Hurreeee!"

Didi looked up into the tree. "Do you have a ladder that can reach her?"

I shook my head. "The ladder at the cabin, the one we'd used for painting, isn't tall enough."

"How could she get so far up that tree?"

Only one answer flashed in my brain. Joey. Somehow, he'd grabbed her, like he did the night of the campfire, and carried her up the tree. Like a hostage. And only one person could make him let her go—if I could get him to come.

I grabbed Didi's arm. "Call Fred. Tell him to bring an extension ladder. And tell him to hurry. I'll stay with her."

Didi dashed back to the cabin as more lightning exploded overhead. I prayed that a bolt wouldn't hit the tree. That my sister wouldn't die like Joey. That lightning wouldn't start another forest fire. That Didi would reach Fred in time.

"Hang on, Robbie. Someone's coming to get you down."

I paced around the tree, talking to her in what I hoped sounded like a calm, reassuring voice. Inside, my gut was in knots and my heart ached with worry. I tried telling Robbyn another silly story, but the words just wouldn't come. The endless minutes dragged on as rivulets of water poured off the field and pooled around my feet. What was taking so long? Did Didi reach him? If he didn't come, how would I get Robbyn down?

Finally, I heard someone coming and splashed forward to meet him.

But it wasn't Fred who showed up. It was Vern.

His shirt, shoes and overalls were soaked, his gray hair plastered across his head. Fear showed in the deep lines across his face as he dropped the extension ladder he carried.

"What are you doing here?" I asked. "Where's Fred?"

Vern shook his head, shouting over the storm. "Fred's back at the cabin with Didi. It was me who left Joey in the tree fort. Fred knew about it, but I made him swear to never tell."

"Tell what?"

"That I took away the ladder. I was mad at Joey."

I let this sink in. It wasn't Fred after all. "You left your friend to die?

"I didn't know he'd get killed. I thought he'd find a way to get down on his own. But I guess he was too frightened. Then it was too late."

Anger pulsed through me. I grabbed Vern by the front of his shirt and made him stagger up to the tree. "And now my sister's the one stuck with no way to get down. You've got to help her!"

He pulled away, his head flung back, scanning the leaves above us. "Where? Where is she?" The vapor cleared. There on a long branch sat Joey, and huddled next to him, Robbyn. She looked so small, her face pale, her eyes wide and fixed in a stare.

Vern jumped back and gasped. "Joey! Is that you?"

Joey put his hands on Robbyn's back and moved her down onto the branch. She cried out and clenched her legs and arms around the branch. She cast an angry glance back at Joey then inched away from him. The branch bowed under her weight.

"No, Robbyn!" I shouted. "Don't move! We'll get you down!"

Her skinny legs dangled and she buried her face onto her arms. "I'm sc-scared!"

Eyes transfixed on the scene up above, Vern braced his hand against the trunk of the tree. "You can't do this, Joey. She's an innocent child."

Joey jerked his fist toward his chest.

Vern nodded. "Yes, yes. Innocent like you." He tried to kneel but his legs gave out. He landed in the mud, sobbing. "I'm sorry I left you. I'm sorry you died. I'm sorry I never 'fessed up. All these years I've been sorry." He hung his head and choked out, "....sorry, sorry."

I cupped my hands and yelled, "Don't hurt her, Joey. Vern has confessed. He said he was sorry. That's what you wanted, wasn't it?"

Joey raised his arms.

A gust of wind full of rotten leaves and debris swirled around us like a small tornado. I watched, helpless, as Robbyn's thin body rolled to the side and swung out, her legs jerking, her tiny hands barely clinging to the branch. As her scream cut through the air, a flash of dazzling white light lit up the scene. The force of the thunderclap smacked me and Vern to the ground. Thunder rattled my bones, leaving me gasping for air.

I thought we were goners.

Just like Joey.

CHAPTER 18

I blinked.

I wasn't dead. Sore and dazed, but alive.

Robbyn sat safely on the ground next to me, crying. She looked unharmed, as if she had just plopped down after tripping on a stone. Vern struggled to stand but he looked like he'd live.

I touched Robbyn on the shoulder. "Are you all right?"

She gazed around as if coming out of a dream. "What happened?"

"Don't you remember?"

"Uh-uh."

Her body shook with shivers. I put my arm around her and got her up. "Come on. I'll tell you all about it later. If I don't get you home and into dry clothes, Dad'll kill me."

The storm clouds parted and a full moon shone down on us as we walked back to the cabin. Vern trailed behind carrying the unused ladder. I kept my arm draped over Robbyn's shoulder, ready to pull her close, just in case. How would I explain what just happened? Who would believe what we just went through?

Lights blazed in and around the cabin. Didi hurried out to meet us followed by Fred.

"Is she all right?" Didi asked as she bundled Robbyn in a warm blanket and held her close.

"Yeah. She's fine," I said. "Joey—the ghost—had her hostage in a tree."

Fred's eyes widened. "Hostage?"

Vern caught up with us, limping a bit. "Joey used her to get me to come."

"I thought it was you he wanted," I added, looking at Fred.

"I kept tellin' you I wasn't there. All three of us kids used that fort. But the day Joey died, only Vern was with him."

Vern sank onto the picnic table bench. His eyes had a faraway look. "When I saw what happened to Joey that day, I was afraid I'd get sent to juvenile detention. I begged Fred not to tell. I never told Anabelle, neither. My pa had a bad heart and needed me to help around the cabin. If I got sent away...well, it would have killed him."

Fred nodded. "It was a secret we kept all these years until you showed up and started askin' questions."

"And burning that wood," added Vern. "Who would've guessed Joey's ghost was locked inside?"

Robbyn peered out from the blanket at Vern. "Was Joey the smoke person?"

"Yes he was, honey," said Vern, patting her arm. "But he won't bother you no more."

Didi steered Robbyn inside to dry her off and get her into some pajamas.

Vern massaged his sore knees, looking worried. "Am I gonna be in trouble about Joey's death?"

"After fifty years?" Fred shook his head. "Don't talk foolish now."

"You were just kids then," I added. "It was an accident. You didn't mean for Joey to die."

"Well, I still feel awful about it. I want to do something to show I'm sorry."

Fred put his arm over Vern's shoulder. "You'll think of something."

Headlights beamed through the darkness as a van crunched to a stop. Dad was back. He loped over to our little group in the yard, his arms filled with packages.

"Man, am ever I glad to be back. Four hours waiting for the road to be cleared." He set down his load and surveyed the group gathered around the fire pit. "Anything exciting happen while I was gone?"

Robbyn came running out of the cabin and gave him a hug. "I got to ride on Rosie and I planted my flowers and the smoke person took me up a tree and Zeke got me down and now we're having a party."

Dad tousled her hair. "You and your wild imagination!"

Vern and Fred exchanged glances.

"It ain't her imagination," said Vern. "It's all true."

And so everyone stayed late to fill him in on what had happened.

CHAPTER 19

Red, white and blue streamers fluttered from every spruce tree around the cabin, making the place look more like a political rally than a birthday party. Robbyn ran in and out of the cabin with settings for the picnic table in the yard. Plastic forks and spoons, paper napkins and plates, all in star-spangled banner harmony.

She seemed totally fine after her adventure with the ghost. Some of her story was missing a few parts, but she talked about Joey like he was her new special friend. Gone was any memory of him kidnapping her to the tree. Even I was having a few kind thoughts about him. He'd sure given us an adventure.

All our friends from Rustic came with gifts. Didi gave her a bracelet woven from Rosie's mane hair. Anabelle gave her a T-shirt with a picture of a trout. From Dad and me, a new backpack filled with colored markers, a drawing pad, and a paint set. But I think her favorite gift of all was from John Begay.

"You have the courage of a bear," he said, handing her a small package. "This is how I see you."

She tore off the paper and squealed with delight when she saw the carving of a bear waving at her. "It's the best!" she said, then planted a quick kiss on his cheek.

Vern and Fred also brought a gift but it wasn't for Robbyn. From the back of Fred's pickup, Vern hoisted a small tree, its roots wrapped in wet burlap. Fred grabbed a shovel.

"I called your aunt Sara early this morning," explained Vern. "I asked if we could plant a tree near the river in memory of Joey. She thought that was a swell idea so here it is."

"What kind is it?" asked Robbyn, touching the dark green leaves.

"It's a cherry tree," said Vern. "Someday, you can pick juicy cherries from it."

Fred picked out a spot with a view of the river and started digging a hole.

While they worked on preparing the hole, Mr. Begay carried a padded box over to the picnic table and opened it, letting the spicy aromas out. "Some treats from my oven," he said.

My mouth watered just looking at the three pizzas he set out. One had smoked trout and dill.

Another had venison sausage and bell peppers. And the last one—my favorite—tomato and four cheeses.

"Let's chow down while they're hot," said Dad, calling Fred and Vern from their digging.

It was the best pizza I'd ever had. One day I was going to build an outdoor oven so I could make pizza at home.

True to his promise, Dad had made Robbyn a birthday cake with green frosting and green sprinkles. Before anyone could say "Make a wish," Robbyn blew out all six of her candles. Then Dad stood up and cleared his throat.

"I have an announcement," he said, tapping his paper cup with a plastic spoon.

Everyone hushed.

"Looks like we won't be staying here this winter after all."

"Because of the ghost?" asked Didi.

"Nope. Because I got the job as science teacher at the middle school."

"Great!"

"Congratulations!"

"Excellent!" I said. "No long bus rides down the canyon in the winter!"

Dad grinned. "It's been interesting, roughing it here with no running water. But indoor plumbing and computer connections are sounding real good. We'll be moving in a couple of weeks as soon as I line up an apartment."

After lunch we gathered around the newly dug hole for the tree planting. Vern placed it gently down while Fred shoveled the dirt back in. I brought over the hose to give the little tree a good soak.

Vern brushed a tear from his cheek as he spoke. "I didn't want Joey's spirit to be tied to that old dead tree any more. If he's still hanging around, this is his new tree. Fresh and green, ready to grow."

That evening, after Robbyn was tucked in bed, Dad and I sat out on the porch listening to crickets in the cool night air. The news of Dad's new job and the move to town was sinking in. In some ways, I'd miss this crummy old cabin. I'd thought it was going to be boring here but it turned out great. I'd have a real adventure to talk about at my new school—if anyone would listen to a ghost story. I had a feeling they would.

Getting back to civilization meant I could fire up my computer and write to my friend Taylor. Maybe he could come up to Colorado and visit. We could play some baseball and catch up. And put our stupid argument behind us.

"Is there a baseball team in town?" I asked Dad.

"You bet. Several Little League teams. You'd have to try out, but you'll do fine." He got up and stretched. "This ghost business has left my brain exhausted. It defies all scientific reason. Guess some things just can't be explained. I'm hitting the sack. You coming?"

"Yeah. In a minute. I have to make a stop first."

As I headed down the path to the outhouse, I saw lights flickering down by the river, like a thousand fireflies dancing around the new little tree. I held my breath and squinted. There in the middle of them stood Joey, smiling, waving goodbye and fading away.

ABOUT THE AUTHOR

Marianne Mitchell is the author of twelve books for young readers. She has been an elementary teacher and a writing instructor, is an avid gardener and now volunteers at local libraries in Tucson, Arizona with her therapy dog. She loves a good ghost story and truly believes that "spirits" can visit the living. Drop in and haunt her at her website: www.MarianneMitchell.net.

Coming soon:

THE GHOST IN THE CONVENT

Read the first two chapters >>>

Preview:

THE GHOST IN THE CONVENT

Chapter 1

"Breakfast is on!"

Jenna Lind ran a brush through her long brown hair then flounced downstairs inhaling the sweet aroma of cinnamon waffles, her favorite.

Her father set a plate in front of her. "Dig in while I tell you my good news."

"It must be good news. You usually wait until Sunday to make waffles."

"It is," he said, rubbing his hands together. "I've got a new project to work on." He picked up his briefcase and set it on the table. "It'll be a real challenge but I think we can handle it."

"We?" Jenna wiped the syrup from the corner of her mouth. She'd never been included before in her father's work. Bill Lind worked as an architect specializing in remodels, designing blueprints, and sketching drawings of the proposed projects. Jenna had her own skills at drawing, but that was just for fun.

"While Mom is away taking care of Gram, you get to come with me to a convent in Arizona."

Jenna's fork clattered to her plate. "A convent? Dad, we're not even Catholic!"

Her father continued stuffing papers into his briefcase. His salt and pepper hair stuck up in places, still wet from his morning shower. "Don't get your britches in a bunch, Jenna. It's only for a couple of weeks so I can make plans of the convent property for the developers. You'll love it. It has ten acres of orange groves to explore, dirt roads for biking, and..." he paused for effect... "rumors that the property is haunted."

That got Jenna's attention. She was a sucker for ghost stories. She had read every book she could find about haunted houses, from Nancy Drew to Mary Downing Hahn. Her skin got all prickly thinking she'd actually have a chance to visit some place haunted.

But the wry grin on her father's face told her he didn't really believe the rumors. Telling her the convent was haunted was just his sneaky way to get her to go along. He knew Jenna all too well.

"I'd like you to make sketches of the convent and grounds. They'll be a great help to keep the memory of the place, in case it all gets torn down." Bill Lind snapped his case shut and tossed a manila folder on the kitchen table. "Here are some photos of the convent and the house we'll live in. Start thinking about what you want to take. We leave day after tomorrow."

"But…" She had no time to protest that all her summer plans would be ruined. Dad was already out the door.

Jenna looked at the old black and white photos spread out on the table. The first showed a two-story Spanish colonial style building, framed by citrus and palm trees. It looked welcoming and peaceful enough with pure white stucco walls, a red tiled roof, and a long balcony running along the top floor. A second photo was of a white stucco house surrounded by well-tended rose gardens and trees. A nun wearing a black robe and veil stood on the front step, arms crossed and hands hidden in her long sleeves.

The last glossy photo was an aerial view of the property. It showed the long convent buildings and the main house nestled in the groves. A dirt road angled to a second house and outbuildings. Beyond the groves stretched acres of farmland bordered by a long canal. Her heart sank. There were no paved streets, no neighborhoods or businesses nearby. She had a feeling this convent must be way out in the country. She flipped the photos over. The date stamped on the back said 'June, 1955.' Her spirits rose a bit. After all, her dad's job was to draw up plans for a new development. Maybe by now the city had built up around it bringing modern shopping centers and movie theatres. Maybe it wouldn't be so dull after all. Maybe.

After landing at the Phoenix airport, Bill Lind drove their rented car to the outskirts of town. The sun was going down, turning the western sky into flaming shades of orange and red. Jenna sighed as the last neighborhood lagged mile after mile behind them. Not a single mall in sight. Not even a lousy convenience store.

He slowed the car and pointed. "There it is. Our project."

The dreary buildings of the convent loomed behind a chain link fence, surrounded by dried up trees and overgrown with tall weeds.

She stared glumly out the car window. "Dad, this place is a dump!"

"Chin up, kiddo. If the place were perfect, I wouldn't have been called in to help."

It needed help, all right. The white buildings were streaked with dirt, several windows were cracked or boarded over with plywood. Red tiles from the roof lay scattered on the dusty ground. Scruffy brown palm trees marked where an old driveway had once curved in from the road.

"How long has it been like this?" Jenna asked.

"The church closed it about thirty years ago," her father said.

"Why?"

"Lack of funds and changes in the Catholic Church. In the '60s fewer women wanted to be nuns in a convent. They wanted to be out, doing social work in the community." He paused and craned his head up toward the bell tower. "This place wasn't always so run down. You saw the photos of how nice it used to be."

"And what will become of it?"

He wrinkled his brow. "That part gets sticky. Some want to tear the whole place down and start fresh. Build a shopping center, condos, maybe a small park. Others want to try and save at least part of the old convent for its historical value. I'm meeting with one of the developers tomorrow morning to go over plans. The developers sound like they're in a hurry to get on with the project, one way or another."

Jenna stared at the convent again trying to imagine what it had been like for the nuns who lived there, sheltered from the world and all its troubles. She closed her eyes, picturing instead a lush, green place with church bells ringing calling the nuns to morning prayers, birds cooing. When she opened her eyes again, she could have sworn she saw shadows of black with flashes of white rippling under the arched walkway. Was she now conjuring up ghost nuns walking the halls? She blinked, shaking off the image. The shadows must have been made by the fading light as the sun went down, nothing more.

Her father turned into a dirt driveway directly across from the convent grounds. It led to a small house. Jenna recognized it at once as the stucco house in the old photo, only now there were no lush rose bushes or smiling nun welcoming them at the front door. Twisted mesquite trees spread their branches above the house. In the fading daylight they offered a lacy canopy of shade. It was blistering hot outside and she longed for a tall glass of iced tea or lemonade.

"This used to be the caretakers' house," her father said. "They moved out several years ago so we may have to do a bit of cleaning up to make it cozy again."

Although it must have been a hundred and fifteen degrees outside, the house felt cooler thanks to its thick adobe walls and the shade from the trees. Jenna walked through a musty living room with faded overstuffed chairs and a ratty sofa. No television in sight, not even an old one with an antenna. Off to the left, a door led to a small kitchen and breakfast nook. Her father flipped on the light switch and a dull fluorescent flickered overhead. "Good. The electricity is on."

While he checked out the kitchen, Jenna looked into one of the bedrooms. By the window sat a single bed all made up, waiting for her.

"The room, OK?" her father asked.

"Do I have a choice?"

"There's a small screened porch on the back side. No AC out there, though."

"Nah, this will do."

He clapped her on the back. "There! See how easy that was?"

Jenna helped unpack the car and find places for their stuff. There were no dressers in the bedrooms so Jenna assumed they'd be living out of boxes for a while. She shoved her suitcase filled with T-shirts and pants over to the wall then plopped down on the bed and flipped open her phone. No service. She snapped it shut, disappointed she couldn't tell her friend Caitlyn about the new digs. "Dad, my phone doesn't work. I can't get connected."

He popped into the doorway holding out his own phone and a blank screen. "Mine, too. Maybe we're in a dead zone."

"It's dead all right. I bet this place is stuck back in time, before cell phones."

"Keep trying. I'm off to find a store for some groceries to tide us over a while. Back soon."

Jenna lay back on the bed and tried Caitlyn again. Nothing. *This was going to be a long two weeks if I couldn't talk to my friends*, she thought. She peeked out the small window by the bed. The room was stuffy so she cranked open the window hoping for a cool breeze. Instead, hot air rushed in like dragon's breath. She cranked it closed again. But as she did, she noticed a light glowing in a convent window. Then it moved to another window, and another. Was someone over there? Her father wouldn't be back for a while and she wasn't keen on sitting around in this old house doing nothing. Curiosity nudged her until finally she gave in. Maybe the ghosts over there just wanted to say hello.

Chapter 2

Jenna followed the chain link fence until she came to the place where it had been cut and pulled away from the post. She had no problem getting through, and judging by the litter of soda cans and chip bags, other snoops had prowled around here before. A flashlight would have helped but unfortunately it was still in the front seat of the car. She'd have to make her way by moonlight.

The double wooden doors of the main building were chained and padlocked, as expected. Off to the left, an arched walkway led to the buildings in the back. Dry leaves skittered across the tiles in a gust of wind as palm branches rattled overhead as if scolding her for trespassing. A long row of doors and windows she passed reminded her of the classrooms back at her elementary school. But with no lights on inside it was impossible to see through the grimy windows. If not classrooms, maybe these had been the rooms where the nuns had stayed.

At the end of the building, the walk took a turn and led her into a garden courtyard. A stone fountain stood in the center, dry of course, the basin filled with leaves, broken twigs, two candy wrappers and a crumpled beer can. Four stone benches bordered the fountain. Jenna sat down and tried to see this little spot as it might have been. It would be the perfect place for her to sketch in the morning. The remains of flowerbeds, dried rose bushes, and a gnarly old vine spoke of a once pleasant garden.

At the far end of the garden several stone slabs, bone grey in the fading light, poked up from the weeds. A chill came over her at once. She edged closer to the slabs, all lined up in neat rows of five or six across. She shuddered, realizing it was a cemetery, the final resting place for the sisters who had given their lives to the church. No fancy decorations on the stones, just simple names and dates.

At the end of the last row she stumbled on a pile of dirt, grabbing one of the headstones before she stepped into an open, unfinished grave. Why was it dug and then not filled in? Who was it meant for? She ran her hand over the mound of loose dirt. Instead of feeling crumbly and dry, the dirt was damp as if it had been newly dug up. Again a breeze riffled through the courtyard but this time it wasn't a hot summer wind. It was ice cold, like winter gust, making her shiver in her shorts and thin shirt.

A voice called out, "Hey!"

Jenna jumped up, jerking her head first one way, then another, trying to locate who or what had made the noise.

"Who's there?" she rasped.

A flutter of wings exploded from the rooftop. *Birds, only birds.* As her heart slowed and her shoulders relaxed, other sounds caught her attention. More voices whispered down the hallways, first mumbling, then sobbing. They seemed to be coming from one of the rooms she'd passed.

Hurrying closer, the sounds shifted to the balcony above her, then echoed from across the fountain. The air swished behind her as if a crowd of people were following her every step. A dark shadow moved along the wall, growing larger and longer as it approached. Her brain screamed at her to run, but her feet refused to move, making her trip on a crack in the walk. As she stood up, the shadow lurched out of the dark and grabbed her arm. She yanked it back.

"Let go of me!"

"Whoa! Take it easy!"

A boy about seventeen with dark hair and dark clothes stood in front of her.

"You scared me to death!" Jenna rubbed her forearm, trying to get a good look at him. "Who are you?"

"I'm Reese. And you?"

"Jenna."

"Why are you prowling around here? It's not safe."

"I'm not prowling. My dad was hired to work on the property for some developers. We're staying in the caretakers' house."

"Developers! They should mind their own business."

"But developing property is their business. And you're here because...?"

"To run off trespassers like you."

"I'm not trespassing."

"Yes, you are."

Hands on her hips, she glared at him. "Who died and put you in charge?" She could see him more clearly now that he'd stepped out of the shadows. He was dressed in jeans and a faded T-shirt with the words Arizona State College on the front. Shaggy bangs fell across his eyes, hiding part of his face but not the serious frown he wore.

He pushed past her. "Come on. I'll walk you to the front."

Jenna wasn't done investigating but this rude boy changed everything. Reluctantly, she followed him. Their footsteps echoed on the tiled walk as they headed for the convent drive. Patches of moonlight cut through the dark, casting a silvery sheen on the dead palm trees. Across from the convent a light glowed in the caretaker's house meaning her father was back, probably wondering where she was. She glanced up and down the dirt road looking for another house.

"Do you live around here?"

He pointed up the road. "Just past the canal."

"This place must have been beautiful once."

"Yeah. It was." He glanced back at the dark buildings. His worried look deepened. "I just wish they'd leave it alone. It's bad enough without developers coming into stir up everything."

"Like what?"

"You don't know?"

Jenna shook her head.

"Something bad happened here years ago. But the sisters hushed it up. All anyone on the outside knew were rumors and stories."

"What kind of stories?"

He snorted. "Ghost stories. Of ghosts trying to scare off the developers with their cries and moaning."

Part of her wanted to admit she'd heard some eerie noises, but she didn't want to let him think she was easily scared. "Old buildings always have funny noises. My dad has been on lots of jobs like this. No big deal."

He started walking up the road. "Suit yourself. But don't be surprised if..."

She jogged after him. "If what?"

"Nothing. Forget it. Just stay out of the garden back there."